A

Arianne Richmonde is an American writer and artist who was raised in Europe. She lives in France with her husband and coterie of animals. *The Glass Trilogy* is based on much of her personal experience—she used to be an actress.

As well as The Glass Trilogy Books, she has written *The Pearl Series, The Star Trilogy*, and the *USA TODAY* bestselling suspense story, *Stolen Grace*.

Hearts of Glass

(The Glass Trilogy #3)

by

ARIANNE

RICHMONDE

This book is a work of fiction. Names, places, characters and incidents are either a product of the author's imagination or are used fictitiously. Any resemblance to actual events, locales or persons, living or dead, is entirely coincidental.

Shards of Glass and *Broken Glass* *(books #1 and #2)*.

A brief synopsis of Janie and Daniel's story so far . . .

Shards of Glass (#1)

Ingénue actress Janie Cole is in love with her director, Daniel Glass. He's controlling, he's demanding, and he's a perfectionist, and Janie wants nothing more than to be his shining star. Tall, dark, and devastating, and with eyes so blue they sear, she cannot get him out of her mind, or her dreams.

Just one problem though: Daniel's married.

But when his wife dies in a coma, and some time later Daniel casts Janie in his erotic romance movie, Janie's fantasies become a reality, and it terrifies her. Her mind, her soul, and especially her body . . . Daniel could take it all, no matter how hard she tries to hold her own.

While filming *The Dark Edge of Love* in Hollywood, Janie's leading man, Cal Halpan, gets fired and none other Daniel Glass is set to be her new leading man, as well as her director . . .

Broken Glass (#2)

Janie collapses with exhaustion from anemia and ends up in the hospital for a brief spell. Filming is put on hold. Janie can't shake off her obsession that Daniel is still in love with his late wife, the invincible blonde bombshell, Natasha Jürgen. Not only that, but rumor has it he's sleeping with half of Hollywood. Janie is determined to keep Daniel at a comfortable distance and their relationship strictly professional, but his insistence, charm, and the power he has over her psyche, wins her over. She simply can't resist.

Because of family commitments, Janie sets off to Vegas, with Daniel in pursuit. Janie finds out that Daniel is far from the player she imagined and she lets herself be his, but just when their relationship is cemented, a calamity befalls the couple.

Daniel is in a coma, and his sister-in-law, the neurologist Kristin Jürgen, appears at the hospital, suddenly in charge of his wellbeing. And the last thing she wants is Janie by his side. Janie is banished from Daniel's hotel . . . worse, she finds out that Kristin Jürgen is married to Daniel.

Or so Dr. Jürgen *claims* . . .

Read on to find out what happens next . . .

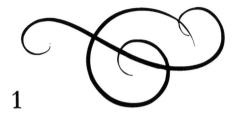

1

Daniel.

THE HORROR OF what is happening to me is beneath my fingertips, but I cannot move them. It is on my breath but I cannot speak. It is before my eyes yet I cannot even blink.

I am immobile.

But my brain is alive. Very much alive. I want to jump up and grab them by the throats—these gatekeepers who are forcing me to be imprisoned in my own body. I was awake. I was well. Janie was with me and it was a matter of hours—yes, hours—before I knew I'd be up and running again. I could taste recovery. But then they medicated me. Medicated me back to oblivion.

This is déjà-vu. I have seen this before. How could I have been so blind? I should have seen it fucking coming. I should have been on my guard.

I cannot move.

I hear her sugared voice. I smell her cloying scent, hovering above, her white coat a reminder of the power she wields over me.

I guess this is it.

I never thought I could be snuffed out so easily, like a flickering candle.

Encased in a tomb of frustration and internal anger, my mind wanders back to Janie. If I could shed tears, they would be for her. I think of her beautiful fragile frame in my arms. Her lovely lithe body spent and sated after I have given her my all. The way she likes to be dominated by me but won't admit it. And now I lie still, dominated by another, someone I now know is pure evil. I am a shell. A soul. I cannot protect myself. I cannot protect the one person I love. I imagine the soft timbre of Janie's voice, Her innocent yet fiery brown eyes, the love pouring from her gaze.

I will never see her again.

I am as good as nothing.

A Year Earlier.

"DANIEL, WAKE UP!"

"What?" A voice that seemed only vaguely familiar lifted me out of my sleep. I rubbed my eyes. My neck was stiff and felt as if someone had cranked it sideways. I'd fallen asleep and, in a brisk moment, remembered where I was: at Natasha's bedside in the hospital in New York. The nightmare flooded back to me; the reality of where I was, the choice before me.

"We need to make a decision, Daniel."

"I . . . I need time," I rasped, my voice barely a whisper. I looked up at Kristin, my sister-in-law. Not just my sister-in-law, but Natasha's neurologist. I barely knew the woman and here we were sharing this horrible fate. There was camaraderie in the misery we were about to endure. Because, even though I had long since given up on my marriage and knew Natasha was in love with another man, she was still my wife, goddamn it, still a part of me.

Kristin leaned over and pushed a wayward lock of my hair from my sweaty brow. "She's brain dead, Daniel. There's nothing anyone can do for her. She's no more than a vegetable. The oxygen—"

"Please stop," I shot back. "I can't do it, alright? I simply can't make a decision to end someone's life!"

"It's what she wanted, Daniel. It's in her last will and testament."

It was true. Who in their right mind would think of stipulating that sort of thing in a will? Well Natasha had, apparently. Drawn up by an attorney, with Kristin as her witness. Natasha had also made her sister the executor, should anything befall her. Kristin in charge of everything despite the fact so much of my own money was part of the various trusts Natasha had set up, including a charity, close to her heart, for orphaned chimpanzees. However coldhearted Natasha had been with me, particularly regarding her extra marital affair with her polo-playing lover Ricardo, she was kind to animals—something that warmed me to her from the beginning. I didn't like the idea of this stranger—her sister—pushing her way into Natasha's life, and wanting to end it just as quickly, yet taking over everything in her wake. Natasha had left her entire estate to her sister, not to me. Including a house I'd bought her in the Hamptons as a wedding gift. A cottage in Bermuda, before, of course, I'd got wind of the fact that she had married me for my money, and in love with Ricardo all along. Yes, I'd been a fool. And a generous one at that.

"What the hell do you want me to say, Kristin? That I'm okay with pulling the fucking plug? Because I'm not, can't you *get* that?"

She held my gaze for a second, a tear sliding down her cheek. "You think this is easy for me? She's my little sister. And I love her. But Daniel, it *is* what it is. I can't change fate."

I was beginning to regret that I'd insisted Natasha come to the very same hospital where Kristin worked, after her accident in the park. It seemed like an innocuous fall, when a bicycle in Central Park careened into Natasha as we were crossing the road. She even got up and laughed about it. Her leg was bruised, but she seemed fine. It was only later that evening she began to complain of a splitting headache, and I called Kristin. She was top in her field—it seemed the obvious thing to do. But I should have picked a doctor outside the family, someone more impartial. Because Kristin was invested in following Natasha's wishes, to a tee. The will I never even knew existed was now being thrust in my face.

5

"Daniel, this was what she wanted. This is what she *wants*."

Now.

THE SCENE STRETCHES before me like a never-ending yawn, my mind frantic but my body unable to respond. I wonder now if Natasha's death could have been avoided. I wonder now if Kristin accelerated—no, caused Natasha's condition. I wonder now what drug Kristin administered to Natasha. Maybe what she did to me she did to her. Because all I know is that I was fine an hour ago, but now I'm paralyzed.

This woman is a shark and I am her prey.

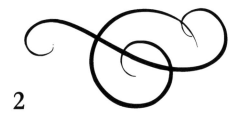

2

Janie.

MY MIND WAS spinning. I could hardly breathe. Standing inside Daniel's hotel, where I'd been living so happily for the last few days, I tried to evaluate what was happening. My mouth was a gaping hole as I painfully swallowed the concierge's words: "*Her first name is Kristin. I believe her name, before she married, was Jürgen.*"

"Daniel's wife?" I asked again, as I leaned against Ethan's front desk to support my Jell-O legs.

His eyes softened. "Look, I'm sorry. But . . . I'll bet you're not the first."

"What? You're saying I'm Daniel's bit of fluff

on the side?"

"I didn't mean it like that. Listen, Mr. Glass is a very wealthy man. As I say, I've only been working here four months so I wouldn't know his extra-marital habits, but . . . look, this is Vegas after all." His tone had changed from reverential and respectful to *we're-in-it-together, you-and-I, isn't-it-terrible-to-be-treated-like-dirt-by-the-rich-and-famous?*

"You know nothing about him," I snapped. "I've known Daniel for years. I've worked with him. I can't believe this is happening!"

"Have you got another place to stay?"

"I'll be fine," I said, my head in my hands as I put all my weight against the desk to stop myself falling.

Ethan came out from behind his desk, wheeling my suitcase behind him. A reminder that I had been chucked out of Daniel's hotel! He took me by the crook of the arm. "Take a seat. Gather yourself. I know some cheap places to stay if you haven't got anywhere else to go. I'm sorry, my hands are tied. I simply cannot sneak you in here or I'd lose my job."

I felt like some sort of cheap floozy. The other woman. I let Ethan lead me to the lobby sofa. My legs were wobbling and I took baby steps in fear of collapsing to the floor.

"I'll get you some water. Just . . . relax, okay?"

Tears welled in my eyes, but I didn't even have the energy to cry. Doubt peppered my mind. Could it be true? Just because Natasha Jürgen had a lover when she and Daniel were married didn't mean that Daniel wasn't hopelessly in love with her. I had lapped up every word he'd said in the plane, on our way to Vegas. Believed him when he told me it was *me* he loved. Believed him when he told me that their marriage had been a sham. He wouldn't be the first man to be in love with a bitch. And maybe he'd missed Natasha so much, he settled for the next best thing: her sister. *No! No! What was I thinking? It was impossible, it had to be! Kristin was playing some bullshit scam!* He couldn't have tricked me like that! Then again . . .

Daniel was a trained actor.

How many women in the world have been fooled by men? How many divorces hinge on the fact that the guy has been unfaithful? Men are used to lying. Men are good at lying. And why should Daniel Glass be an exception?

But then, by turn, guilt hammered in my heart. Here I was accusing the man I loved, a man who couldn't speak for himself, nor defend himself. It wasn't fair that I was doubting him like this, when I knew nothing of the circumstance. Maybe Ethan was lying. Then again, why would he? What had he to gain?

"How do you know Daniel and Kristin were married?" I demanded. He handed me a glass of water. "Just taking her word for it?" I said, and then: "Anyone could pretend that she was Daniel Glass's wife."

His look was one of pained sympathy. "Because I was at their wedding. Well, not at the ceremony, but you know, I organized the party afterward. They all came back here."

The word "wedding" took the oxygen clean out of my lungs. My heart was thumping through my chest cavity so hard, it echoed. "Wedding? What, here in Vegas?"

He nodded. "If it makes you feel better, Mr. Glass was pretty drunk. The whole party was."

I grabbed the sleeve of his jacket. "Who else was there? When was this?"

"Like, two months ago. The truth is though, I never saw Mrs. Glass again until today. She was in a hurry. Came by like a bat out of hell, packed up your stuff and gave me strict instructions not to let you up. I'm sorry, but you know, the jealous wife thing is pretty common around these parts."

Again, the intimacy of a man I hardly knew talking to me as if I were the jilted girlfriend and he my confidante. Not the Ethan of the past few days who had been treating me like royalty. *Was* I the jilted girlfriend? If so, what the fuck had Daniel been doing just a few hours earlier, proposing to me when he came out of his coma? But then again, he *had* been in a coma, hadn't he? Maybe he wasn't sound in the mind. Perhaps he *had* married Kristin and was playing the field. Maybe the rumor about him *was* true . . . that he *had* been running around fucking Natasha Jürgen lookalikes because, hey, *who could look more like Natasha than her Doppelgänger sister Kristin??*

I shakily got out my cell phone and clicked on Google. I had never checked out Kristin. Whenever I had looked in the past, she had been no more for me than a passing piece of information, a mention on Natasha Jürgen's bio on Wikipedia:

She was raised in Springfield, Connecticut, with her older sister, Kristin, now a neurologist.

I clicked on Kristin's name, expecting something to come up. Not a bio as long as Natasha's, obviously, but still . . . why had I never done this before?

But her name wasn't clickable on Wiki. Nothing.

My fumbling fingers managed to type her name into the Google search bar. This was the first thing I saw:

Sunrise Hospital and Medical Center's neurologist Kristin Jürgen M.D, has earned an MDX Most Compassionate Doctor Award. MDX allows patients to nominate their doctors as being one of America's Most Compassionate Doctors.

Kristin Jürgen graduated Bennington College in Bennington, Vermont. She earned her M.D. at the University of Medicine and Dentistry of New Jersey, where she completed her residency in neurology. Kristin Jürgen also finished a fellowship in neurorehabilitation at the Hospital of Joint Diseases under the auspices of New York University in New

York City, N.Y. She is board certified in neurology and now practices primarily at Sunrise Hospital and Medical Center, and Silver State Neurology, both in Las Vegas.

Dr. Jürgen is honored for her initial and precise follow up care, as well as her bedside manner. She has also received the 2013 American Registry MDX Patient's Choice award and has been featured in Nevada's Monthly "Top Doctors."

So she was the real thing, not some quack. Worse, she was revered as being some fucking saint with her patients. There was no way I'd convince anyone otherwise. No wonder she had been able to pull her weight at the hospital. She had obviously complained about the nurse, Barbara Mendez, and had Dr. Bellows transferred, pulled strings to make sure she was in control of looking after Daniel. Doctors in high places could do these sorts of things. Who knew? Maybe she'd fucked the right person to get what she wanted. Actresses did it all the time, why not doctors too?

I read on, hoping for some mention of her personal life.

Nothing.

I thought of how Daniel was fine one minute—he'd woken up! And the next he'd regressed into a coma again. Coincidence? There was no doubt in my mind that Kristin had induced his coma after he had woken up. They could do that sort of thing with drugs, although usually it was for the *benefit* of the patient. I Googled for more information:

A patient can be put in a medically induced coma with the administration of barbiturate drugs or by lowering the body temperature to 32-34° C. The purpose of an induced coma is to allow the brain to rest after an injury, such as those that deprive it of oxygen (a blood clot, a blow to the head that caused pressure in the brain to increase, or a chemical imbalance in the nerve cells, resulting from a drug overdose). Doctors can bring the patient out of a coma by discontinuing the treatment.

I couldn't think straight. I needed something to eat. My head felt light, and when I tried to stand up, I nearly blacked out from dizziness. I drained the rest of my glass, trying not to splutter water all over myself.

"Have you got any place to go?" Ethan said. The way he asked me made me instantly suspicious. He was on Kristin's payroll, and I didn't trust him an inch. I needed to get Daniel out of Kristin's clutches, but how? One thing was for sure: Kristin Jürgen had some sort of ulterior motive tucked up her sleeve. If she really was his wife, I assumed she stood to inherit his entire estate, the value of which didn't even bear thinking about. Daniel was a billionaire. He played it down, never alluded to his wealth, nor boasted about it, but everyone knew that his father had left him a vast empire that had mushroomed from a car parts' industry to God knows what other investments and companies. Daniel was a savvy, smart man, and I could only imagine how clever he'd been with his investments.

"I'm fine, Ethan. If you just let me sit here for ten minutes while I gather my stuff. Please, go back to your desk, I'll be okay."

"Let me know if I can do anything for you."

I watched Ethan as he made his way back to

his desk. I lay my suitcase flat on the floor, unzipped it and rummaged through my belongings. I needed my $25,000 Bellagio chip because my bank balance was pretty low. I'd have to find a hotel to stay. Food, et cetera. Thank God Daniel had taken me gambling because, I reminded myself, the big contract for *The Dark Edge of Love* that I had been negotiating with my agent Cindy Specktor and the producers, was still not signed. If the job didn't go ahead—and with the way things were with Daniel it looked as if it wasn't going anywhere—I hardly had a penny to my name. Luckily, the chip was still tucked at the bottom of my makeup bag. I wondered if Kristin had seen it, would she have pocketed it?

I sent a text to Star; I didn't want Ethan to hear what I had to say about Kristin. I sent the same message to Pearl Chevalier, despite what her assistant had told me; that she and Alexandre were AWOL and would not be taking calls for two weeks during their "no contact" vacation:

URGENT! Daniel woke up from his coma. He was fine. His sister-in-law Kristin Jürgen is his new neurologist and has kidnapped him

and induced him into another coma. Please believe me, I am not imagining this. She drugged me and is dangerous. They say she is Daniel's wife. I think she wants to kill him. Help! Please call me back.

I pressed SEND but when I re-read the text I realized how nuts I sounded. Even Star would think I'd lost the plot. So I added another text for Pearl. Maybe this would grab her attention:

P.S. Kristin Jürgen has stolen your pearl necklace.

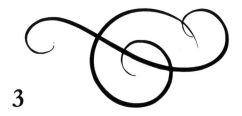

3

Daniel.

"YOU REMEMBER, HONEY, don't you?" Her voice is sickly sweet as she sponges my immobile body. I am floating on a raincloud, almost as if I can see her from above. But the lump that is my torso, legs and arms like appendages that are nothing more than blocks of wood attached to my being, are immovable. The person lying here is not me.

And yet it is. There is nothing I can do. Nobody can hear my inner screams.

I am shaking my head, yet my head is not moving. I'm yelling "No!" Yet no sound is emanating from my lips, nor my throat. "*No, I don't remember, you bitch, because what you're telling me is a lie!"*

"We got married, Daniel. You were very, very inebriated. You remember? You came up from New York to spend a weekend here, have some fun. We went out for dinner. You ordered the most expensive wines on the list and had the sommelier running around like a blue ass fly trying to please you. Where was it we ate? Joël Robuchon's, wasn't it?"

"Stop lying!" Again, my lips sealed as I mentally shout. We had a brief dinner to discuss Natasha's various charities, but nothing more. I went home. We parted ways.

As if reading my mind, Kristin says: "You just can't remember a thing, can you, you stubborn man? You blacked out after your fourth whiskey. You suggested we go to a chapel. You were coming on to me, Daniel, flirting like crazy, saying how much you missed my sister, even if she had treated you like dirt underneath your fingernails. I don't blame you. Everyone was in love with Natasha. You think it hasn't been challenging for me all these years having her to compete with? All my life she was the beautiful, talented one. She was smarter than me, so I had to study around the clock to get ahead. I had to have *something* of my own. Show Mom and Dad that I was special. She was always so goddamn blessed, so adored. You know my hair isn't even blond? The day I was old enough to color my hair, you bet I did. Mousy brown, that's me. I even had liposuction on my thighs and a nose job. Who wouldn't have wanted to look like her? She was gorgeous. It was always Natasha this and Natasha that. The golden child, the pretty, talented one."

The sponge is hurting me as Kristin scrubs my genitals with vigor. I think of Janie, how skillfully she had my dick in her hot wet mouth, and now this lunatic attacking my private parts like I'm something to be dissected on her laboratory operating table. I miss Janie. I miss her touch, her smell, her sweetness. I try to disassociate myself from the present reality and let the memories of beautiful Janie surge through me in a blissful wave. My only solace. I inhale the scent of her soft, sensual skin, my nose pressed between her silky thighs. I have her pussy in my mouth as I taste her juices, flicker my tongue on her clit and carry her to another mind-blowing orgasm. Her hips lose control as I hold her tight ass in my hands, bringing her even closer to my mouth. Her spasms and her cries have me more turned on than I have ever been in my life with a woman.

"Isn't it crazy that you and I were able to get married just like that?" I hear Kristin's fingers snap to emphasize her point. Snapping me out of my reverie. "Only in America. Vegas really does cater to the lowest denominator of human being. I mean, imagine that! That all we had to do was show up with a witness in tow, and you and I were married five minutes later! I know, honey, you can't remember, and well, I was going to do the right thing and get this union annulled. Because we never even consummated our marriage. We were both too sozzled to have sex. We hadn't even been in touch since our wedding—God knows, I was too busy with my research work. And then you had this accident, slipping on the floor, and I knew that I was the only person with the right skills to look after you. I didn't want anyone interfering. So, you know, us being married is a good thing."

She maneuvers my body so I am now lying on my side. Her voice rattles on. "What a crazy coincidence. Two people close to me falling into comas! And both times my being in the right place at the right time. What are the odds of that? Millions to one! That's why I know this is all meant to be. I'm becoming quite the coma specialist. Fascinating. And you really have enhanced my life. The two of you. It's such fun being this rich! Natasha was more than generous in her will. Sorry you missed out on that. And I had no idea quite how loaded you are, Daniel. How come you don't flash your money around more? I mean, seriously, baby, you should have been having *fun* with your wealth. If I had your looks as a man, I'd be lining up twenty women at a time, partying more! And there you were, hanging out with that skinny little actress with the big, brown, innocent eyes—like I can really imagine how much of a sport she must be in bed, that is, if you even got that far with her. Cute, but clueless. Not like Natasha. She was a *real* woman. Such a shame her life was cut so short!

"Shut the fuck up, you nutter!" my grey matter screams.

"Did I just see you twitch, Daniel? We can't be having that now, can we? Got to keep you nicely tucked up in your coma until I figure out what your future holds. Because I have been toying with the idea of administering a drug to make this wiener of yours stand to attention, although right now isn't the best time of the month for me. And I'll need to administer some fertility drugs for myself first. After all, I'm no spring chicken. I mean, at forty-two it isn't easy. And I always did want a child. Or do you think having a baby would be too taxing at my age? I have to admit, the idea of being woken up to breast feed in the middle of the night is hardly appealing. Actually, it's pretty gross. I'll need to mull this idea over first. No, you know what? I don't think having a baby would be a good idea after all. And I guess, when I'm in charge of your money—well, the money that the greedy trustees aren't controlling—I don't really need you to be around at all."

I can swear I hear myself groan but Kristin's verbal diarrhea cannot be stopped.

"You may be asking yourself why I need the extra money. You think I like just being a doctor? Okay, it *is* a prestigious job and the pay isn't bad, but it's not about that . . . I want fame, Daniel. I want to discover a cure for Alzheimer's or muscular dystrophy. I want to be a medical star, go down in history books, in scientific journals. That's why I need extra money, don't you see? I need my research projects funded. It's like God is on my side. He wants me to succeed. That's why I inherited Natasha's money." She laughs. A raucous, secret-joke sort of laugh. "Shall I tell you a little dark secret? Maybe I'll hold on a little longer until I know what to do with you. Then I can let you in on my secret. Well, okay, I'll tell you. Why not? You might even find it funny . . ."

She lowers her voice to a conspiratorial whisper: "Wait . . . someone's coming."

4

Janie.

AS I WAS tucking the Bellagio chip deep into my jeans' pocket, my cell rang. For some reason it made me jump out of my skin. I was tired, jittery, and starving hungry. It was Pearl Chevalier. I heaved a sigh of relief.

"Pearl, thanks so much for calling back."

"It's not Pearl," the stranger's voice said. She had a French accent.

"Oh, hi," I replied. "Pearl's not there?"

"I'm her niece, Elodie. Alexandre's niece."

"Hi Elodie, yeah, Pearl once mentioned you to me."

"Pearl's on vacation with my uncle. She left

her phone behind."

I was amazed that a woman in Pearl's position would forget her cell, but then I remembered the "no contact" policy.

"I know you, Janie," Elodie said.

I had no recollection of meeting Elodie, but I didn't want to be rude. "You do?"

"I saw you in *Where The Wind Blows.* Crazy, but I feel like I know you personally."

That happened to me a lot. Being an actor means you are familiar to complete strangers. It isn't uncommon for people you've never met before to be telling you their darkest secrets. You are their friend, their confidante. In this instance, though, being Elodie's friend wasn't a bad thing at all—I figured it would help me get in touch with Pearl.

"I read your text," Elodie continued. "That's why I'm calling you back because it looked important. I'm going to find out more, but I think my mother has mentioned this woman Kristin Jürgen to me. And not in a good way. Her name sounds really familiar."

I told Elodie the whole story, trying to keep my voice down so Ethan wouldn't hear. It unnerved me to be revealing all this to a total stranger, yet at the same time, just sharing all my troubles gave me a sense of liberation. I understood as I spoke, though, she must think it was all really far-fetched. There was silence on the other end of the line. I wanted to scream with frustration. Nobody believed me.

"I can help you," Elodie said, finally. "You have no idea the kind of shit I've had to deal with in the past." *Deal wiz in zee past,* her accent said. Cute. Just knowing that someone, anyone, was offering to help me, lifted my spirits. Although I'd been hoping to reach out to one of the Chevalier's hotshot attorneys, not Alexandre's niece.

"Have you been to the cops?" she asked.

I rewound the Kristin saga in my head. This super-successful neurologist who had received awards for being such a fabulous doctor, and me, the love-struck actress accusing this respected neurologist of trying to murder the man I was in love with. I knew any normal policeman would think I was crazy. "Not yet. My story sounds so nuts, I'm not sure if they'd believe me." I glanced over at Ethan, who was stealthily eyeing me up and down. *Damn, I wonder if he's heard.*

"Good. Don't call the cops for now—I'm sure we can sort this out," Elodie advised.

"Hang on, don't go anywhere, hold the line." I zipped up my case and made for the door, wheeling my suitcase behind me.

"Wait up! Miss Cole, let me call you a cab," Ethan shouted after me.

"I'm fine, thanks, I'll get one on the street. Elodie, are you still there?" I struggled through the swing door.

"Where are you right now?" she asked.

"Outside Daniel's hotel, which I've been asked to leave. Look, I need a lawyer."

"Sounds to me like you need a bodyguard, first and foremost."

I smiled. Her accent was adorable: *'first and foremost.'* She had a point about my needing a bodyguard, considering the fiasco in the hospital with Kristin.

"No, seriously. I'm going to make a call," she said.

"Is there any way you can contact your uncle? Or Pearl?"

"Believe me, every contact my uncle has, I know about. He and I are very close. You want help? Look no further, I'm your girl."

La Femme Nikita? I admired Elodie's bravado, but wondered how much of it was B-S. But I was hardly in any position to turn down help. Why hadn't Star called me back?

"I'm going to hang up and make some calls," Elodie said. "Meanwhile, I'll send a text message, which you need to respond to. This way, I'll know where you are, so don't, for fuck's sake, lose your phone."

I frowned. "What are you saying, you'll know where I am? You mean if I call you?"

"Your cell will be like a GPS the second you return my text. I can keep you traced. Keep your phone with you at all times. Never leave it lying around. Got that? I'll call you back." She was gone. A few seconds later a text came through that said, **It's me.** I replied, **Thank you,** and felt relieved to know that Elodie had my back. She was quite the sleuth, and I wondered how the hell she knew all this undercover stuff. I seemed to remember Pearl telling me she was in her early twenties, around the same age as me, but I couldn't recall what she told me Elodie did for a living. Although with an uncle as wealthy as Alexandre Chevalier, I guessed she never needed to work a day in her life if she didn't want to.

I hailed a cab and went to the Bellagio. I cashed in my chip. I had never in my life carried that kind of hard cash in my purse, and it terrified me. I wanted to deposit it in the bank but didn't have time for all that now. Every second was ticking, and I needed to find Daniel. I assumed Kristin had moved him to a different wing of the hospital.

I checked into a room, right there at the Bellagio—after all, I could afford it now. I grabbed some snacks from the mini bar and took a lightening-fast shower. I shoved the cash and my valuables in the room safe, then left.

I punched in Elodie's number. She was fast to pick up.

"I was just about to call," she said. "Sorry it took so long. You okay?"

"Worried sick about Daniel."

"Paul is on his way."

"Paul?"

"The bodyguard I'm sending. Ex cop. He knows the law. He has contacts with the Vegas police and NYPD. He's your man. He can go with you to the hospital and you'll be safe. Wait for him outside the main entrance to the Bellagio. Meanwhile, I have a private detective on the case. She's finding out stuff about Kristin Jürgen, looking into the marriage with Daniel and checking out her past. Well, to be honest, my girl's not an *official* private detective, as such. Better than that. A Hacker. A good one, too. And a very fast worker. She can find any shit out in the blink of an eye. I'll keep you posted. Remember, keep your phone close to you at all times."

"How will I know what Paul looks like?"

But Elodie had hung up. I called her back but it went to voicemail. I assumed she was on the line with the hacker.

"Miss Cole? Janie Cole?"

I turned around and to my relief a man was standing before me. *Fast work!* He had a friendly, open face but looked tough enough to protect me, although slimmer than I had imagined a bodyguard would be. I saw my reflection in his mirrored sunglasses. I looked harrowed, my face gaunt. I still hadn't had time for a proper meal, not even a sandwich.

"Paul? You're Elodie's . . . um . . . friend?

31

You're here to protect me?"

"That's right," he answered with a smile. "I've been sent to protect you."

"Thank God you're here. We need to get to the hospital."

"Yes, we do," he answered smoothly. "Come with me."

I followed him to his car that was parked in the valet section, although he hadn't given anyone his keys. His walk was a swagger, his big black boots and buzz-cut a testament to his tough demeanor. He looked as if he'd walked off the set of a TV cop show. A movie star type of ex-cop, not an ex-cop you'd expect in real life. He opened the back door for me, and I slid in. He was taciturn but polite. I guessed bodyguards were trained to be that way. The strong silent type.

"So how do you know Elodie?" I asked, settling into my seat.

"Through work." He started the engine and drove out of the hotel parking lot.

"You work for her uncle too?"

"I freelance. Got a lot of clients but don't tend to discuss them, if that's alright with you."

"Sure," I said, a little unnerved. "You know

where we're going?"

"Absolutely."

There was something in the way he said, "absolutely" that should have given me the first clue. I looked out of the window at the Strip passing by us. Nervously, I fumbled in my purse for my phone. I wanted to call Elodie, check this guy was who he said he was. Actually, he hadn't even introduced himself at all! I'd simply assumed things.

But when I pulled out my phone, my heart tumbled to my stomach and rocketed to the floor. It was out of goddamn battery! Had I brought the charger? Of course I fucking hadn't! Maybe Elodie had called. My stomach churned.

"Paul, do you use an iPhone, by any chance?"

"No, a BlackBerry."

"You don't have one of those generic phone chargers, do you?"

"No, ma'am, I don't."

"Damn. Can we quickly stop at the Apple Store, please? Or somewhere I can buy a phone charger for my iPhone?"

The locks on the door clunked shut. All of them. Simultaneously. I knew I was in serious danger. Oh, fuck! Adrenalin spiked through my veins like heated gasoline about to burst into flames. "Paul" did not answer. He just looked in his rearview mirror, his head slightly cocked, his reflective shades giving nothing away of the probable menace in his eyes.

"Excuse me, did you hear what I said? I'd like to stop and buy a phone charger, please."

"I heard you," he replied ominously. He kept on driving, a faint smirk edging his sculpted lips. All I could think of was what an idiot I'd been. A fucking moron to get into a stranger's car! Had my mother not warned me about that ever since I was two years old? I hadn't checked the man's credentials. I had assumed. *Never fucking assume, Janie,* I berated myself. *You idiot!* Ethan had obviously got wind of things. Maybe he'd even had me followed to the Bellagio. After all, duh, I'd hailed the cab right outside Daniel's hotel door! I hadn't even been followed probably, but the cab driver himself may have been summoned by Ethan/Kristin in the first place. I'd just walked right into their trap! *Assuming* this man was Paul. Then my mind double-tracked back and forth. What if Pearl Chevalier had left her phone at the hospital when she came to visit Daniel, along with her pearl necklace? What if "Elodie" was not Elodie at all, but Kristin, putting on a fake French accent? I felt dizzy. Intrigue and paranoia engulfing me, smothering me like a heavy wet blanket. Then I realized I was being ridiculous; if Pearl had left her phone at the hospital, I would have found it. Of course it was Elodie I'd been speaking to . . . but still. Whatever the scenario, I was up shit's creek.

"Where are we going?" I demanded, rattling the door handles that were holding me prisoner. I tried to buzz down the windows, but of course they were blocked too. "Stop this car! Right now! I want to get out!"

But he just ignored me and carried on driving.

And the dead battery on my phone wasn't going to help me. There was no way Elodie could track me now, because my cell wouldn't be sending a signal anywhere. I let out a furious gasp. I'd been a fool and all I could do now was try not to panic and keep my wits about me.

5

Daniel.

I AM STRUGGLING to keep my mind active, even though my body is shut down. I think of the only thing that keeps me going: Janie. The second that girl came into my life I knew she was special. A wisp of a thing, with big brown eyes, a fiery disposition, and an intractable will. She wanted to please me. I tried to go easy on her, attempted to treat her like the rest of the cast, but she got under my skin. I knew right away that she was falling in love with me. I was getting married to Natasha—blinded by her glamour, her stardom, the promises she made me of a blissful future together, yet this little actress was determined to knock down my barriers, unravel the truth. So many questions about her role in *Where The Wind Blows*. She challenged me, made me think.

"Who am I?" she'd say. "What's my motivation?"

"That's for you to find out, Janie. "That's what rehearsals are for."

"I know who my character is and where she's coming from, but you, as a director, don't seem to be supporting that. I see her as—"

My mind is struggling with this memory that now won't play out. Did she say these things to me? Or is it my imagination? Another recollection slips in where the other fades . . . The first time I realized I wanted to fuck her. Yet I was married. Having racing thoughts about my cock in her mouth when I had a wife to go home to. An unfaithful, cheating wife, who didn't give a damn about me.

Scott, the actor playing Janie's lover in the play, was leaning over her, whispering in her ear. I had told him to play it that way, yet a twinge of jealousy gripped my heart. In a physical way. Like an actual stab. I could feel a vein throbbing in my temple. A vein I had never known lived there. For the first time ever in my career I compromised my vision. "It doesn't work after all, Scott. Lose the tender words. At this point in the story . . . well, trust me, it isn't working. See me after rehearsal, Janie, I want to have a word." My cock ached for this willowy girl. I wanted to take her, fuck her up against the wall backstage, splay her little pussy open with the one part of me I couldn't control. I imagined how tight she'd be, how ravenous for me. I felt so turned on I knew I had to have her. That it was a matter of time. It was obvious how much I needed her. I already knew how much I liked her as a person, respected her as an actress, but it was then I knew how much I desired her. Wanted to make her mine.

I picture her now, in my arms . . . no, beneath me. I have my mouth on her lips and I'm telling her that I am irrevocably in love with her. "You are my world," I tell her. She has her legs wide apart, and she's moaning, the tip of my cock poised at her sweet, taut opening. She's squirming beneath me, whimpering, "Please Daniel, I need you, I need you inside me." I tell her that I know she needs me, and that's why I'll never leave her, and I push myself in, into her soaking, welcoming little pussy—tight and hot—just a little, just enough to feel the crown of my cock expand and pulse, and for her to urgently buck her hips at me. I make tiny little movements, telling her I'm crazy about her, how I love being so close, how fucking her is my greatest pleasure in the world because we are one: one whole, one heart. My words are her aphrodisiac. The more sweet talk I make, the wetter and wilder she gets. I pull out and start prodding and massaging her clit with my erection. I'm kissing her mouth, her eyes, her neck. I'm rolling one of her nipples between my thumb and forefinger, tugging gently. She's practically crying, her arms squeezed around my back, as they move down . . . frantically, lustfully to my ass. It's adorable how she thinks she has the strength to force my buttocks down, closer to her groin. She's pummeling me, pinching her little fingers into my taut flesh. It's my cruel torture . . . to make her so wet, so desperate to be fucked . . . but to make her wait. I like to control her pace, because that way, when she climaxes, thunder rolls inside her body and breaks her into a million imploding stars.

"I'm going to come," she groans, "I'm going to come if you keep teasing me like this." I tell her that we'll come together, and I drive myself further inside her, rocking my hips just the way she likes it, so my pelvic bone hits her clit on every thrust and my cock massages the base of her opening. The rhythm is now like a metronome, and I know at what point she'll come. Her lids are fluttering in a stupefied daze . . . her eyes are rolling back. I'm in really deep now . . . in every respect. I want to be with this girl forever. I'm in deep and there's no return.

It's when I cup my hands under her buttocks, hold my hips still for a second and then push to the back of her womb that she starts screaming my name. Her legs go stiff, sweat beads trickle down the small of her back. I bring her even closer to me . . . closer and never close enough. My lips are on her ear. "I love you, Janie, I love you so much." She's coming hard, her pussy clenching my cock like a limpet on a rock, as if her life depended on never letting me go, and my orgasm powers through my erection in a wild, desirous rush.

We are in this together. Until death do us part. That's right . . . I forgot . . . Death . . . that's the word *du jour*, the word on everyone's lips. They are talking about me . . .

I'm being shaken out of my beautiful home movie by doctors discussing their trade. Unpleasant images and words sift in and out of my consciousness, ruining my dream:

"Nonhuman primates are used as experimental models to study a wide range of human neurodegenerative diseases."

I hear Kristin's voice chiming in. "We used human microarrays to profile genes from brains of human, macaque, and marmosets, and combined this with available data from chimpanzees and orangutans to create a data set that provide salient similarities and differences in expression of genes underlying Alzheimer's, Huntington's, and Parkinson's diseases."

My mind is fading fast. I hear more rumbling voices all around me. More doctors discussing my fragile state. But I can't decipher their words . . . their mumbling recedes to a gentle hum. My brain is blanking to a pale white . . . a light is shining in the confused orb of my brain. Yet I feel strangely at peace.

It won't be long now.

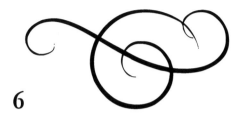

6

Janie.

I HEARD MUTED screams and cries. Not human. Relentless. Piercing. Begging cries. But coming from another place, somewhere distant. I couldn't work out where I was. I remembered being at the Bellagio. I could hear my stomach rumble. My head was light. Dizzy. All I could think of was food and how hungry I was. I pictured a French baguette with Brie and lettuce, mayo, and tomatoes washed down with a soda. I licked my dry lips. I was thirsty too. I peeled my eyes open but could barely see. It was dark. I was lying on a sofa, fully clothed. Where was I?

Then I remembered. The car. The man whom

I thought was the bodyguard, sent by Elodie. Kristin. Daniel in his medically induced coma. My cell phone out of juice. I could hear my own muffled sobs. Sobs of defeat. I was too exhausted to even stir. I mentally scribbled a note, a proverbial message in a bottle:

I'm alone in the dark, locked up, with nobody to hear my cries. They've taken him from me. Nobody believes me. She is a liar, a thief, and a fraudster, and probably a murderess. She'll kill him for sure.

Not only does she want me out of the picture . . .

She wants me dead.

But then I heard a shuffle. I wasn't alone after all.

"Who's there?" I groaned. My head hurt. I lifted my hand to my forehead and traced a small lump just above my left eyebrow. Bruised, but not cut.

A light went on, illuminating the dank room. I guessed it was a basement.

"I wondered when you'd wake up. Hungry?

Thirsty?"

I lifted my eyes and saw the outline of the man who'd abducted me. He was no longer wearing his mirrored shades. His eyes were black—a Johnny Depp kind of soulful black, and his five O'clock shadow spoke of time passing. How many hours had gone by? I hadn't noticed stubble on him before. I must have been here for ages. What was he doing here? My watchdog? What the fuck was *I* doing here? Had he hurt me? I needed to get to Daniel!

"What am I doing here?" I fired at him.

"You're being kept out of trouble, is all. You didn't answer my question. You hungry? You must be, you've been out for a good forty-eight hours."

I didn't have the energy to ask more questions. "Yeah, I'm starving," I conceded. "Thirsty too. What have you got?"

"There's a kitchen. I could fix you a sandwich. Or grill you a steak."

My food fantasy daydreams popped straight out of my mouth: "I want a baguette with Brie, please. Pickles if you have them. Lettuce, tomato. And a Coke. Classic."

He laughed. His laugh told me he wasn't much

older than me. "Not demandin' one bit, are we little princess?"

"What is this place?" I asked nervously, my mind a blank as to how and why I was here. "Where am I?" The last thing I remembered was being in a car with this guy.

"I'll fix you a cheese sandwich. Nothing fancy. And we do have Coke. Not classic, this isn't the Ritz." He chuckled again. "You're cute, but you know that, right?"

"So they tell me," I said, feeling my bruised lump again. "I suppose I've been abducted and you're taking me hostage?" I asked, trying to sound cool although my pulse was racing with dread and apprehension of what was to come.

"Abducted, yes. Hostage, no. I'll fix you that sandwich. By the way, you bumped your head in the struggle. I didn't hit you, in case you were wonderin.'"

"A real gentleman," I said wryly, not remembering a thing.

I must have momentarily dozed off, because what must have been a while later, I awoke to the smell of processed cheese under my nose.

"Here, eat this." The guy put a plate out, and

the soda on a table beside the sofa. I sat up, or tried to. He helped me, positioning his hands around my waist and hoisting me vertically. His shoulder brushed against my cheek. He smelled of cedar wood, or some expensive cologne, which surprised me. The intimacy of his proximity was unnerving.

I delved into the sandwich, moaning with relish as I chewed. The feeling of real food hitting my stomach calmed me, instantly giving me strength. I gulped down some Coke.

"Better?" he said. I nodded, filling my mouth with another large bite.

"We got TV," he told me. "But otherwise nothin' else to do. Except fuck, if you want to."

I stopped chewing, wondering if I'd heard him right. "No thanks." I sounded cocky but my heart was thundering in my chest. I'd been dismissive of him, he'd rape me for sure, to punish me. Or strike me. But I also know that if I showed fear I'd be giving him what he wanted—and he'd rape me anyway, probably even more violently.

But to my amazement, he laughed again. "You don't know what you're missin.' Most girls beg me to fuck 'em."

"I'm not most girls," I shot back through a full mouth. My sassiness was working. It was keeping him at bay. "Where's Daniel?"

"The guy in the coma?"

"Yes, the guy in the coma. He's still alive, right?" The man didn't answer. "What do you know?" I shrieked, my voice an octave higher. I grabbed him by the T-shirt and felt a set of hard abs beneath the fabric. This guy obviously worked out. A lot. *Easy, Janie, don't get too over confident, this man could break you in two . . . in more ways than one.*

He held me by the wrist, restraining me. "Do that again and you'll make my dick hard."

I looked him square in the eye. But I was terrified. Just as I suspected . . . getting hysterical was turning him on. I kept my voice calm, even. "Tell me where Daniel is."

"And you'll fuck me if I do?"

"No, I won't fuck you. And if you fucked me, I'd lie there like a stone. If that would give you pleasure, go ahead. Although . . . if I were in your shoes? I'd want a woman to reciprocate." I eyed him carefully, and he said nothing. I guess I'd gotten to his pride. A cute looking guy like this would be used to women chasing him. This was

Vegas, there was no shortage of women who'd find a crass, but physically attractive guy like him sexy. "I just want to know," I carried on, "how much she paid you to bring me here, because if you let me go, I can double your fee." I mentally thanked God for the Bellagio chip money. "I need to find Daniel, my boyfriend. My fiancée, actually."

"Now I know you're shittin' me, 'cos he's married to Dr. Jürgen."

"Ah, so you *are* working for her? Thanks for the confirmation. I question that, actually—their marriage. Daniel would never . . ." I didn't finish my sentence. The truth was I didn't really know who Daniel was. Not the whole of him, anyway. There was the seed of doubt germinating in my mind. Maybe he'd made a foolish mistake and *had* married Kristin, in a moment of weakness? "Anyway," I continued, "the woman is a crazy monster! Not to be trusted. Her sister died after being in a coma while she was in Dr. Jürgen's care. Coincidence, don't you think? *Not*. She's a whack-job who needs to be stopped, and if you have any conscience whatsoever, any morals, you will let me out of here and lead me to Daniel!" I was crying now, the thought of Daniel lying there, helpless, was too much to bear.

My keeper swept his hand over his dark hair. "The dude is in a coma, there's nothing any of us can do. And anyway, you're barkin' up the wrong tree, lady, cos no, I don't have any morals and I don't have that much of a conscious either."

"Conscience, not conscious," I snapped, gulping down my tears.

"Whatever."

"You think a coma is that straightforward?" I demanded. "Even patients in a supposed 'vegetative state' can know what's going on around them. I read about a team of neuroscientists that used state-of-the-art technology to communicate with a man in a vegetative state. He was able to relay information to them about his condition, saying that he was not in any pain. Not verbally but by studying and mapping the neural patterns flashing on their screen. Like a 'yes' produced a different neural signature than when he thought 'no.' You see? He is *not* a lost cause! I am not giving up on Daniel!" I hoped my little speech had convinced this man how urgent the situation was. I drained the last of my Coke and sprang up from the sofa. An instant head rush caused me to topple back down, landing with a thump on my coccyx.

"Whoa, be careful." His hands shot out to steady me. "Easy, baby, you don't want to bash your head again."

His word, 'baby' filled me with fury. How dare he talk this way to me? My eyes were daggers, my twisted mouth poison. "You make me sick," I mumbled, "doing something like this for money." I wanted him to hear me, but at the same time talking to him this way was risky. All I could think about was getting to Daniel, but I was probably going about it the wrong way.

"It *was* the money, I admit. But being holed up in here with you gives me a *whole* lot to look forward to." He smirked. "Get it? *Holed* up? A *hole* lot to look forward to, as in a *'hole'* to look forward to? Your sweet pussy bein' that succulent little hole." He laughed again, his straight white teeth making me wonder why he was involved in shady dealings when he could have practically found work as a fashion model.

I screwed up my face as if I'd eaten lemons and cockroaches all in one go. "You disgust me," I muttered. I looked around the room for a weapon. My purse was hooked on the edge of a wooden chair. It wasn't that heavy though. I wished I'd been wearing spiky heels, but my Converse sneakers were useless. There were no ornaments, no lamps, no fork or knife accompanying the sandwich he'd brought me. The room was sparse, except for this sofa, a table, two chairs, and one of those oversized beanbag loungers on the floor.

He stroked my cheek with the pad of his thumb. "You and me will fuck, baby, you'll come a thousand different ways, then you'll forget about this Daniel dude, I guarantee." He took my empty plate and glass away, and swaggered toward the kitchen, and I instantly regretted that I hadn't thought of smashing them over his dumbass head.

There was no point arguing with this half-witted jerk, nor trying to convince him. So far, he hadn't manifested a violent side, but that didn't mean I was safe. He was strong and muscular and could overpower me with his little finger. I needed to find his Achilles' heel, or win him over in some way to get the information I needed, without compromising myself.

And get the hell out of here.

7

Daniel.

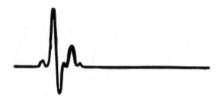

A KALEIDOSCOPE OF colors is fragmenting my brain into puzzle pieces. I am trying to fit them into the right places. I see my father, and my childhood dog, Smokey. They're waiting for me, calling my name. It's getting brighter now, a white light looming around my head like a halo.

A then a burst of pale gold engulfs my whole body . . .

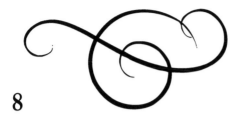

8

Janie.

I GOT UP from the sofa—slowly this time—
and cased the room. The exit door must have
been in the kitchen, where the guy was right now. I
realized I'd never asked him his name. I found him
washing up my plate. His tall frame towered over
me.

"Hey, gorgeous," he said, winking at me.

The exit door was right in front of me.

"Don't even think about it," he warned, reading my mind. "It's locked and I have the key."

"What's that noise?" I asked.

He cocked his head. "I been wonderin' the
same thing."

"Where does this door lead?"

"Corridors. Laboratories. This is where Dr. Jürgen works."

I pressed my head up against the door. "Sounds like a bunch of animals. Locked up animals."

"You freakin' me?"

I looked at him. "She's a neurologist. You know what they use animals for, don't you? Vivisection? Experiments? But I guess if what you said is true about not having any morals, you wouldn't give a damn."

"Fuck!" he said. "I knew I shouldn't have gotten myself involved in this!" His face changed from menacing man to concerned guy in a heartbeat. For the first time, I felt hopeful. This man did have a heart after all. Maybe I could persuade him to let me go.

"What's your name anyway?" I asked.

He covered his hands over his face. "I can't do this shit. You serious? You think that's animals we hear? Locked up in cages? Monkeys and shit?"

"It sure sounds like it. Look, whatever your name is, you don't have to do this. Keep me here against my will. Like I said, whatever she's paying you, I'll pay you double."

He stared at me, eyeing me up and down. His tough guy demeanor all at once left him as he let out a long sigh and slumped his shoulders. "Fine, let's get the fuck out of here. I promised I'd keep you here until he was transferred to another hospital—"

"Daniel?"

"Yeah, Daniel. Dr. Jürgen wanted me to keep you here—keep you from doing mischief. Nobody was going to get hurt, least of all you." His accent had suddenly become normal, no longer the working class tough guy with an attitude.

I felt the lump on my forehead. "So what about this?"

"You bumped your head getting out of the car."

"So why can't I remember? Why are the last couple of days a blank?"

"Because Dr. Jürgen gave you something. I don't know what it was . . . an injection of some kind. Something to knock you out till you were safely locked up here. Look, she told me to distract you . . . entertain you. Get into your panties if I could. Told me how you were obsessed with her husband and stalking him. She didn't want to call the cops on you but wanted you out of the way. She told me you were a danger, not only to yourself, but to her husband Daniel. She was scared you'd pull out his tubes or something. I thought I was doing everyone a favor."

"Wow, she's really deranged, that woman. She's the one who's likely to pull out his tubes! And I cannot believe that Daniel is her husband!"

He shrugged. "I'm sorry, I don't know who to believe."

"Oh, because she wears a white coat you should believe *her*? She's a fucking lunatic! She drugged me once before. Daniel had woken up from his coma—I was there—yet suddenly he was out like a light the second she came on the scene. Her sister was married to Daniel before she died. He proposed to me! He would have told me if he'd married her. Daniel and I are in love! We're engaged!"

"Look, Janie. Dr. Jürgen is a real doctor. I saw her in action at the hospital. Met nurses and other doctors who work for her. She's the real thing, not some phony. You? You I don't know from Adam. All I can do is take her word for it."

"Well her word is *bullshit,* please believe me!" I yelled out. But the way he was looking at me showed me that he *didn't* believe me. Not one bit. I tried another tactic. "How much is she paying you?"

"Ten thousand dollars."

"That's it? Ten grand? For breaking the law?"

"Hey, I don't know where you come from but ten grand for a couple days work is pretty darn fine by my standards! Got to pay my bills, you know."

"So what are you, anyway? A security guy? A bodyguard or something? How did she find you?"

He raked his hands through his dark hair. "You think I look the part then, huh?" He grinned at me.

"The part?"

"Yeah, you think I'm doing a good job of acting like a tough guy?"

I stared at him. This was surreal. Who the hell *was* this person? "You never did tell me your name," I said suspiciously.

"Remy. Remy Foxton."

"You say that like I should know who you are."

"Maybe you seen me on TV."

"You're a fucking *actor*? You're kidding me, right?"

"No."

"So all that pussy talk was you . . . you—"

"Playing a role. Glad I had you convinced."

"How did she find you? Put an ad for an audition in Variety, looking for actors or something?"

He laughed. The movie star, pearly white teeth laugh that had me so flummoxed earlier. The actor thing made total sense.

"Okay, truth is I'm not really a real actor. Yet. But I wanna be an actor. They tell me I got the looks for it. I'd really like to stop this line of work, but like I said, it pays the bills."

I narrowed my eyes, thinking of the last time I got tricked by an actor. "Cal Halpan didn't have anything to do with this, did he?"

"Cal Halpan? Sounds familiar."

"We worked together on a movie. He was my leading man. Daniel was the director actually."

Remy grinned. "You're an actress? Get outta here!"

"Remy, *can* we get the fuck out of here, please?"

He squinted his eyes as if sizing me up. "You can make up the ten grand I'll be losing if I let you go?"

"I swear. Like I said, I'm a woman of my word; I'll pay you double."

"Twenty grand?"

"Twenty grand."

"Deal," he said, and held out his hand. We shook on it. "You'd better come through, I have some major debts to pay off." He dug into his jeans' pocket and pulled out a set of keys. "Your ticket to freedom."

I exhaled a giant sigh of relief, and tears prickled my eyes. Finally, there was a chance to find Daniel before it was too late. "Thank you. Thank you so much."

I watched him, as he fed the key into the lock and turned it, like I was a dog observing its owner eat steak. Every second felt like an eternity while Daniel's life was on the line. I knew I had to get him away from Kristin but wasn't sure how. I still had no plan. It was bad enough that Kristin was such a respected doctor, but if they really had gotten married that would give her legal right to make executive decisions. How the hell would I—

a nobody in people's eyes—convince anyone?

"Are you as strong as you look?" I asked Remy. "Or are those muscles just for show?"

He laughed. "Yeah, I'm pretty strong."

"Can you fight? Do you have any martial art skills?" I wasn't sure what the hell I was thinking, but trouble, in one form or another, was surely on its way.

He unlocked the door and it flew open. The animal sounds became instantly louder. I winced.

"I box," Remy told me. "I'm pretty tough for real, but in a ring, not on the street. I'm sure as hell not looking for trouble, nor do I want to do anything illegal."

"Oh, so locking me in here wasn't illegal? You had no—"

"Ssh, what's that sound?"

"All I can hear are the animals, I—"

"Ssh! Listen," he whispered.

There was someone there, at the far end of the corridor. My heart jumped into my throat and then plummeted down to my toes. I thought I heard the cock of a revolver. And then, out of nowhere a slim, dark figure emerged from the shadows. "Don't move," the voice said.

I recognized the accent. "Elodie?"

"Thank fuck," she replied, moving towards us. Elodie looked like a cat burglar. Not that I'd ever met one in the flesh. Even though I recognized her voice, I was spooked by her. Dressed all in black, her face covered by a mask.

"Who the hell—" Remy began.

"It's okay," I broke in, gripping his arm with my clawed hand. I hadn't realized how tense I'd been. "She's a friend."

"With a fucking gun? I'm outta here!"

But Elodie was right before us now. "You're not going anywhere, Remy Foxton." She pointed a pistol at his chest.

"How the fuck d'you know my name?" he gasped, his hands in the air. I wanted to know the exact same thing. How did she even know where we were? With my cell phone battery dead?

She grabbed me by the wrist. "Turn around, Remy. Hurry up, you guys, we need to set these poor, suffering animals free."

That was all very well and good, but right now Daniel was my number one priority.

As if reading my mind, Elodie said, "Daniel's fine, by the way. We can deal with him next. And sorry about the fuck up with my bodyguard Paul not getting to you soon—."

I cut her short. "You know where Daniel is?"

Out of the shadows four figures dressed in black—also in ski masks, and holding powerful flashlights and huge bolt cutters—shot into my vision. I jumped back. One of them muttered something to Elodie in French. Three of them looked like men: chunky, muscular. Another was slight, could have been a woman. More hushed words were spoken in French. I only understood the odd phrase.

"Dépêchez-vous." 'Hurry up,' the thin figure said. I was right, the voice told me she was a woman.

Elodie pushed Remy in front of her, the pistol wedged in the small of his back. I couldn't believe she was doing this. The niece of the respected Alexandre Chevalier behaving this way? Was she covert? Was she working for the FBI or something? I doubted it. Vivisection wasn't illegal. Setting lab animals free was.

"Move," she instructed Remy. "And don't try anything crazy."

"It's okay," I said, coming to his defense, "he's

cool."

"Nobody who works for that bitch is cool," she snapped. "There's an alarm, which we need to disable. Just . . . let's keep in a tight group while the team work their magic."

"Who are these guys?" I said, under my breath. I was terrified of the real Vegas police busting in on us. Any second now. I wouldn't be much use to Daniel if I was arrested and locked up in jail.

"French Foreign Legion. Friends of my uncle's. Don't worry, we'll be out of here soon."

I had visions of wild primates roaming the streets of Las Vegas. Setting lab animals free, willy-nilly, when many of them had never known freedom, was not the brightest idea. They'd get run over by cars and could be a danger to the general public. Chimpanzees could be extremely aggressive and dangerous when frightened.

"Take your gun out of my back," Remy said between gritted teeth. "I'm on your fucking side! I'm working for Janie now. Tell her, Janie. Tell her that you're my new, temporary boss."

"It's true, Elodie. I'm giving him twenty thousand dollars because he let me go."

"Well that was a waste," she said with a snicker. "I was seconds away from picking that lock to free you, myself."

"Don't worry," I assured Remy, "I'll still pay you what we agreed. I'm good for the money."

We waited while the team in black set to work on disabling the alarm system and slipped an electronic card into the lock of a huge metal door. The animals were now hysterical. I was afraid the whole world could hear.

"Ere, take zeez," one of the men said to me above the deafening noise. He hurled a pair of thick leather gloves at me, and a couple of black, nylon masks. "And you, too" he instructed Remy, throwing another pair his way. "You need to protect your 'ands. Zey'll bite and scratch, zeez chimps are fucking strong."

"A shipment of them came in a few days ago," Elodie said. "There should be twenty-six in all."

"Came in from where?" Remy asked, putting on his mask, and then gloves, which reached half way up to his elbows.

"From the animal sanctuary, the one Natasha Jürgen's foundation was funding. Dr. Jürgen's been using them for experiments and breeding. Trying to find a cure for Alzheimer's and other brain diseases. Can you believe she actually gets a government grant for this shit?"

I could feel the pulse pounding in my temples.

"Every year in the U.S., and in France, and fucking everywhere," Elodie continued, looking at Remy, "millions of animals are used in biomedical experimentation and product testing. Experimental drugs are pumped into the poor creature's stomachs—even though the U.S. Food and Drug Administration reports that animal tests have a 92 percent failure rate in predicting the safety and effectiveness of pharmaceuticals. It's sick! Especially nowadays when you've got stem cell research and there's so much advanced technology. Toxicity tests using human cell cultures are two to three times more accurate than tests on animals."

"I hear ya, you're preaching to the converted," Remy agreed.

Elodie lowered her gun. "So you *are* on our side?"

"Paul McCartney is my grandmother's hero."

Elodie gave him a high five. She turned to me. "Get your mask on Janie, and your gloves. You'll need them."

I was horrified at what was before my eyes:

several chimpanzees had shaven heads, with metal electrodes attached to them like helmets. It looked like they'd had holes drilled into their skulls, with these metal restraint devices screwed in, and electrodes actually inserted into their brains.

I couldn't bear to look so I closed my eyes, but the image was imprinted in my brain. It was the most horrendous thing I'd ever seen.

"Don't worry, the electricity's been cut— reason why we got flashlights. We can snip the wires connected to their heads without harming them," the woman said in a thick French accent, amidst the noise. "The vets will take this shit off them later, after they've been sedated. The papers will call what we're doing 'an act of terrorism,'— but *this* is fucking terrorism."

My gaze roamed the room; there was what looked like a monkey fetus in a jar labeled "liquid nitrogen." I glanced at a set of study notes pinned to a corkboard. My eyes scanned quickly:

Cerebral Concussion and Traumatic Unconsciousness Correlation of Experimental and Clinical Observations on Blunt Head Injuries:

Single unit activity in the frontal eye field was investigated in unanesthetized chimps during eye and head movement. Two types of cells (I and II) were found.

I could feel bile creeping up my throat, and I swallowed it back down. My knees felt like water. *What kind of monsters test on* **unanesthetized** *animals?* Monsters like Kristin Jürgen, all in the name of science. Sadly, she wasn't the only one who thought this ethical, obviously. These notes, all typed up officially, were proof that others found this perfectly acceptable.

The next half hour was a fever of activity, flashing past me in a surreal dream. Or better said, "nightmare." At the same time as all this horror, I prayed that Daniel was okay. If this woman was capable of this, she'd be capable of anything.

I followed orders as we made a human chain from the lab to an open back door, where a truck was waiting. The team freed the cages from their positions in the lab, the screaming chimps inside, rattling on the bars, thumping their chests, terrified. Or maybe they were excited and knew we were here to help them. It broke my heart to see the condition they were in. It was pandemonium. The sound was unimaginable, screeching ringing in our ears. As well as the chimps, there were five Beagles. I wondered why I hadn't heard them barking. And three cats, also with electrodes screwed into their heads.

"They've had their voice boxes removed," Elodie explained, "so nobody can hear them howl and scream in pain."

Looking out the back door, I saw that the lab building was isolated, far from the city. It was pitch dark, no lights, and I couldn't see any other buildings nearby. No wonder they chose a place far away—people would be horrified if they knew what was going on here.

"Where are they all being taken?" I asked.

"To a private sanctuary in Utah. My mom's, actually," Elodie said, nodding at the other woman. "Well, she set it up."

"Your mom?"

"That's her," she told me, pointing to the slim figure, who was shouting orders at everyone in French.

I'd heard about Sophie Dumas. Alexandre Chevalier's sister, co-CEO of Hooked Up, the multi-billion dollar social media company, bigger than Twitter and Facebook combined. I couldn't believe she was involved in this. She was risking her career, risking her reputation. Any moment now a SWAT team could come crashing in on us with high precision rifles. My heart was pounding so hard I thought I'd end up suffering a coronary attack. All I wanted was for this to be over with so we could get to Daniel. The idea of us all being arrested before we had a chance to find him was terrifying, consuming my every thought.

But in no time all the animals were loaded, cages and all, and the truck was on its way with the team inside, minus Elodie, Remy, Sophie, and me.

"Let's get the fuck out of this hell hole," Sophie hissed. "Follow me."

We bundled into a waiting SUV. I was glad to see, even in the dark, it had tinted windows. I heaved a sigh of relief as we screeched away, leaving the lab behind, hopefully never to return.

"How did you find me?" I asked Elodie, when we were at a safe distance from the lab. I looked at my hands, still in their gloves. I was trembling like crazy. The screaming chimps' faces were engraved on my mind.

"My hacker."

Sophie chuckled. She was in the front seat, next to the driver. She took off her mask, shook out her mane of thick dark hair. She was a very beautiful woman. Fine featured, with feline-shaped eyes. "Why don't you just come clean, Elodie, chérie? You should be proud of your skills." She turned to me, "Takes after my brother ('bruzzer' her French accent said)—very smart with computers." (Smart wiz computers.)

Elodie shrugged her shoulders. "Okay, I admit, I hack too. I have a small team—we work together. We don't do bad stuff, you know, we only use it for the general good."

Sophie laughed again. "Especially when the general good is to our advantage."

"But my cell phone battery died," I said, confused. "How did you know where I was?"

Elodie pulled off her mask and ruffled out her long brown hair. She didn't look like her mother at all, but she was equally lovely. Her oval shaped face delicate. She didn't appear like a typical "bad" girl, but quite the sweet ingénue. Butter wouldn't melt in her mouth. The last person in the world you'd imagine a hacker to be.

"I picked up the place where your cell's last signal was sent out and located you. Luckily, there are CCT cameras all over Vegas. Found the car on camera and tracked you down. Meanwhile, discovered all sorts of shit out about Kristin Jürgen and her evil practices. Good thing I picked up Pearl's phone the other day, eh? Thanks to you, Janie, we freed these animals."

My mind was still reeling. "What about Daniel?"

"He's stable. That's where we're going now."

Stable. I closed my eyes, silently thanking God that he was still alive.

Sophie chimed in, "Kristin Jürgen will be meeting us there."

"What?" I said, alarmed.

"If what you told Elodie was true, that she's the one who induced his coma—then she'll need to reverse it. She has his medical details on file, too—can't be too careful. If this isn't handled with care, he could wind up dead. Plus, I want to see that bitch, face to face."

Adrenalin cursed through my veins. It was true, Daniel's life was at stake. Freeing him would be no joke. We'd need specialists there, and nurses.

There was no way I'd trust Kristin Jürgen. "But she'll never agree to helping us," I protested.

"Yes, she will," Sophie assured me. "You watch. She'll be taken by surprise."

What lay ahead terrified me. Elodie and her mother were outlaws! I admired them for their convictions, their courage, but now I was involved in . . . in . . . I couldn't even find the right word for it . . . the whole thing was madness. But I didn't have a better alternative. No Plan B.

I was completely out of my league.

"We need the law on our side," I suggested, "if we have any chance of rescuing Daniel. Neurology specialists, too."

Sophie glanced over her shoulder at me and shot me an irritated look. "You think I hadn't thought of that? Relax, Janie," she said, her voice calm. "I have means. I have a fuck-off team of professionals, don't you worry."

I'd heard that expression, "fuck-off" as an adjective. A British-ism. It meant incredible, unparalleled.

"By the way, Kristin's 'marriage' is total bullshit," Elodie chipped in. "No record whatsoever of a union with Daniel. She has no legal right to call the shots as to what happens to him. Wishful thinking on her part, I guess, so she'd have control of him and his fortune. Maybe that had been her plan: to fake a marriage. Anyway, we didn't find anything."

"But Ethan, the concierge at Daniel's hotel, told me he'd been a witness," I told her, remembering what Ethan said about Daniel being drunk, and how they'd all come back to his hotel to celebrate.

"Yeah, he's on her payroll, Janie, bet he told you all sorts of bullshit just to scare you off, get you out of her hair."

I felt flooded with relief, but seconds later, anguish settled in my gut again. How would we pull this rescue off? Anything could go wrong. *Everything* could go wrong. I was with a team of irreverent, law-breaking French people, who did things their own way. I wondered if Pearl had any idea what her sister-in-law and niece were up to. Or Alexandre, for that matter.

"What's the plan?" I ventured. I didn't want to sound ungrateful, but my confidence was waning.

"*Maman* has an attorney friend who owes her a big favor," Elodie said. "US government level.

Also a neurosurgeon and a neurologist whose credentials make Kristin Jürgen look like an amateur. They're part of our plan, don't stress it." She whispered in my ear, "I don't think you understand quite how powerful my mother is. The contacts she has."

My fears were alleviated. Somewhat. "Why are you helping me like this?" I asked under my breath. "And Daniel? You don't even know us."

"*Maman* wants that bitch to go under, for personal reasons, not just on behalf of the animals."

The car raced along, swerving around potholes. We were getting nearer to the city.

Sophie turned around and glared at us. "My ears are burning, are you talking about me?" I could feel myself flush. Then she smiled. "Talk away, I'm going to put some music on." She chose a classical piece . . .very strident and dramatic, which fit the occasion perfectly. I recognized it as one of Wagner's symphonies, but not sure which. It reverberated through the car as we shot through the dark night.

I finally took off my protective gloves. My hands were no longer shaking like they were about to fall off. I held Elodie by the forearm to catch her attention. "What 'personal reasons?' " I murmured.

"Sophie's wife—you may have heard of her—the actress Alessandra Demarr?"

I nodded. She was a major movie star and had been in the *Stone Trooper* films that Hooked Up Enterprises had produced, with that grease-ball Samuel Myers. A huge commercial success that had earned them millions. I knew that Alessandra Demarr was gay and was dating Sophie Dumas, but I had no idea that they were actually married.

"Anyway," Elodie continued, "Alessandra used to be great friends with Natasha Jürgen. They did a couple of movies together. She *adored* Natasha. Alessandra knows for a fact that the sisters never got on. Natasha hated her sibling, yet P.S., Kristin inherited Natasha's fortune. Alessandra thinks something fishy went down. Definitely. But she hasn't been able to prove it. You calling Pearl's cell phone was lucky . . . really lucky I picked up. It led us to her. Alessandra and Sophie knew about the chimpanzee sanctuary—that it had supposedly been left to Kristin—and Alessandra was convinced she was up to no good."

"How did you get the rescue organized so

quickly? The French Foreign Legion team?"

Elodie whispered in my ear again. "When you're as loaded as my mother, and as crazy as she is, mountains get moved, believe me. She could move Everest if she put her mind to it. Plus, my uncle got on the case; he organized the men."

*So this **was** considered an emergency and worthy of interrupting his vacation.* I only hoped that Daniel's wellbeing would also be deemed as important. I lowered my voice so only Elodie could hear. "But your mom didn't have to be personally involved tonight. She could have just paid others to do the dirty work for her."

"Saving these animals is not dirty work, Janie. This is a cause my family strongly believes in."

I felt ashamed of what I'd just said. "No, of course not. I get it. She wanted to be hands on."

The Wagner was drowning out our hushed conversation. "My mom," Elodie went on, "has lived on the edge her whole life. She doesn't do 'safe.' She likes breaking the law and playing hardball with criminals, politicians, and God knows who else. That's who she is. My uncle isn't much better. If Pearl knew half the shit he gets up to . . . well, let's just say he and my mom are crazy mavericks . . . birds of a feather." She bit her lip as if she'd already said too much. Perhaps what had happened tonight was making her more open with me than she would have normally been. After all, I was a stranger to her. How could she know to trust me?

I mulled over what Elodie said before. "You think Kristin forged Natasha's will, or something?"

"Believe me, *Maman*'s got a bunch of heavy attorneys on the case. Handwriting forgery experts too. In the past, Kristin Jürgen was Alessandra's bone of contention, but because of the vivisection thing, my mom is now out for her blood too. Whatever Kristin did wrong, *Maman* will make it her business to find out."

"Wow, your English is good. Where did you learn expressions like 'bone of contention?'"

"From Pearl. We talk a lot, and she always corrects my English. She and I are very close."

"She seems like a really cool person," I observed. "So they have a good marriage, then, Pearl and your uncle?" Why I was so curious, I wasn't sure. The couple seemed so golden and perfect it didn't seem real. I wanted to have what they had, with Daniel. But surely there was a catch? Too 'fairy tale' to be true.

"The best. Still crazy in love after all these years. Although he'd drive me loopy if he were my husband."

"Really?"

"You know, he's pretty jealous . . . possessive . . . can't keep his hands off Pearl. Once I made the mistake of sleeping in a hotel room next to theirs. Bad move, I didn't sleep for all the noise they made. And if she's out of town, working, he calls her ten times a day, monitors her every move."

"Lucky woman."

"Oh, I don't know, I like to be free, you know? Don't like a man to be too all over me."

I noticed Remy had been staring at Elodie rapturously, ever since she took off her mask and revealed her beauty. Maybe he was taking note of what she was saying. I could tell he was smitten. His 'pussy' talk with me had been a total act. Now that he was confronted with a woman he truly liked—for real—he was dumbstruck. Especially as she had been ignoring him. I bet, with his good looks he wasn't used to that. He'd hardly said a word since we'd been in the car. Then again, I think we were all suffering from shock at what we'd witnessed tonight, and what we'd been involved in, firsthand.

Images that would haunt us for the rest of our lives.

9

Daniel.

"YOU KNOW, DANIEL, it's all very well gathering information from the chimps—they've been extremely useful to our studies. But there's nothing like a live *human* to compound our theories. I think I should start monitoring your brain, don't you? My aim is to help mankind understand the human brain *better*. For the good of all. I mean, chimpanzee and human brains are different in many respects. For example, the chimp brain is smaller, and has far fewer neurons; some brain regions are less developed than in humans, some are overdeveloped; some regions present in humans are not present in chimps at all. Some of our animal experiments, to be honest, Daniel, have been a total waste of time."

I thought I'd met my Maker, but I can smell Kristin again so I must be alive. The sweetness is overwhelming. Sickly. Her hands are caressing my head, stroking my hair, tracing themselves around my scalp as if measuring it.

"To understand the human brain, Daniel, we have to know what the brain *does*: its high level emergent behavior. We need to understand how a genetic mutation, or the wrong positioning of a protein in a cell affects behavior. How a drug acting on a specific molecule can produce changes in cognition. You, Daniel, my dear, could be my breakthrough! There was a reason why God sent you to me, don't you think?"

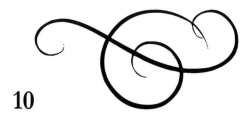

10

Janie.

I THOUGHT I would somehow be involved in freeing Daniel but was not "invited" by Sophie.

"Are you crazy?" she said as the car approached the Bellagio. "Kristin Jürgen already has a bee in her bonnet about you, obviously, or she wouldn't have locked you up. The last thing we want is to rock the boat. She doesn't know me or Elodie, so we're coming along as 'nurses.' We want this to go as smoothly as possible, Janie, no hysterics into the mix."

My mouth dropped open. What a bitch! I'd always heard that about Sophie Dumas, that she was a tough cookie and didn't suffer fools gladly. But I was no fool! I knew how to behave. I wanted to be there when Daniel woke up.

"There won't be any hysterics on my part," I assured her, trying not to feel riled.

"Elodie will keep you posted," she said. "And you, what's your name again?" She cut a daggered glance at Remy.

"Remy."

"You might as well leave now, too. We don't have time to ferry you back to wherever you came from."

Remy opened his mouth to say something but then stopped himself. He looked at Elodie wistfully. "Can I take your number?"

"Janie has it. You'd better go, we need to get on with this. Don't either of you call me, wait till I call you."

We both got out of the car, feeling rejected. It showed in Remy's downcast head and the tears welling in my eyes. They could screw the whole thing up and I wouldn't be there to help . . .

Or hinder . . . I had to admit Sophie was right. I could make things worse for Daniel and ruin everything, just with my presence.

Before I clunked the door shut, I said, "These doctors you're meeting with, are they—"

"They're the best in their field. Now go, Janie," Sophie snapped, "we can't waste any more time."

REMY AND I SETTLED into my hotel room, waiting for room service to bring us a midnight snack Actually, more like a full-on supper. While he enjoyed a stiff whiskey—straight up—to calm his nerves, I was mindlessly flicking through TV stations, desperately trying to keep my mind off what could go wrong with Daniel. My fingers fumbled, every once in a while, to my now fully charged cell phone, but I had to force myself not to call Elodie. I listened to a bunch of messages that had piled up: my dad, Will (who said he felt so much better), and several from Star, apologizing for not having phoned earlier, that they had a new puppy who'd chewed up her phone. Of course the messages had become more and more frantic, and the last one—sent this afternoon—announced that she was here in Vegas, looking for me, and if I didn't get back to her soon she'd call the cops.

I texted her:

Don't call back, about to go to bed, but am alive and fine. Will explain all tomorrow, may need your help. Am at The Bellagio, room 716.

What Star could do for me, I wasn't sure. I had learned one thing: even the rich and famous couldn't solve every problem. It was like throwing a life vest to Daniel in a raging storm. Yeah, there was hope, but no guarantees. I felt myself biting my lip nervously—so hard I could taste the metallic tang of blood.

I looked at Remy, "Won't Kristin get suspicious that they're meeting past midnight? That's not normal procedure in a hospital. And what about the rest of the staff?"

Remy took out his cell. "You want me to call Kristin and check how the land lies?"

I shook my head and laid my hand on his to stop him from dialing. "Tempting, but no. That could really screw things up. Kristin would ask you to explain yourself, for starters. Where are, and so on."

"Yeah . . . of course . . . how dumb of me." He laughed at himself and stretched out his arms above his head. "Never said I was the brightest crayon in the box."

I got up from my position on the bed, went to the mini bar and poured myself a Coke. "You're really taken with her, aren't you?"

"Who? Elodie?"

"Good luck cracking that exotic nut."

"Crazy, huh? She held a gun to my back, and now I'm having ideas about dating her. Like that red flag wasn't enough!"

"Interesting women those two. Quite the mother and daughter team. Although I read that Elodie is Sophie's step-daughter from her ex-marriage, not her biological daughter."

Remy took a swig of his whiskey. "She's fucking beautiful, that's for sure." He paused, then looked me in the eyes and said, "Look, Janie, I apologize for treating you the way I did."

"You did what you thought you had to do. Oh by the way, I've got your money here. It's in the safe."

He shook his head. "Nah, I can't take your money. Not after what you've been through, and I was partly responsible. You must have been scared shitless. And what with Daniel still being in his condition. Not to mention the shit that went down with the animals—that's something neither of us will forget in a hurry. Keep your money for something more deserving."

"But a promise is a promise."

"Really, I wouldn't feel right."

There was a knock on the door. Room service bringing us a feast. Remy tucked into a steak and I had grilled sole with new potatoes and asparagus. I was finally having a healthy, hot meal, after days of cookies, potato chips, chocolate, bad coffee, and too much soda from vending machines.

We stayed up late, me a nervous wreck, and Remy not leaving my side. I guess he knew he needed to keep my mind off Daniel, because every now and then I'd break the conversation and burst out crying. Remy did a wicked Christopher Walken imitation to distract me. I couldn't help but laugh.

Finally, when it was obvious that nobody was going to call us, Remy said he was going back to his apartment. We promised to call each other if we heard anything. Meanwhile, all we could do was try and get some sleep.

After what seemed forever and—as the sun was coming up—I dozed off.

11

Daniel.

"I T COULD BE another twenty-four hours."

A male voice is drifting in and out of my consciousness. Other voices, too, join in. I can't smell Kristin anymore—I feel at ease. I'm surprised I'm still alive.

"Midazolam is a Benzodiazepine and the longer a Benzodiazepine is used, the higher the risk and the likelihood that Daniel is getting addicted to it. Therefore, getting him out of this coma may have some challenges, namely withdrawal symptoms and therefore a gradual weaning off the Midazolam, which might delay his 'waking up.' "

"Withdrawal?"

"I'm afraid so. And when he does come to, there may be side effects such as aggression and confusion because of it."

I feel myself fading again. Floating . . . floating, on a white puffy cloud, comfortable as a feather cushion.

"JANIE, IS THAT YOU?" My voice is different. A growl. Am I dreaming, am I awake?

"Sir?"

Yes, that's right, my name's Finn. I'm Janie's Dom. But she's not called Janie. The name of the character she's playing is something else entirely.

"Sir." She sounds as if she's being gagged.

I look down and am glad to see I've got my sweet little pet just where I want her—where I need her. On her knees, my cock stuffed into her hot pretty mouth. Oh, fuck, yeah. She's sucking me hard as my hips move back and forth. Her delicate little hand is cupping one of my balls and she's groaning, being rewarded with my dick for being a good girl. No lollipops for her, just my huge great cock, which she devours with gusto. She's doing well, drawing on it, sucking in her cheeks, just the way I trained her . . . oh yeah, now she's licking along the shaft, flicking her tongue on my big, wide crest, rimming the head . . .

I groan with pleasure. "Good girl," I encourage her. "If you keep this up I'll let you come later. I'll fuck you from behind, the way you like."

"Oh God," she mumbles. I can turn her on just with my words.

"Don't talk or I'll take away that privilege. That's right, make me come, baby, make me detonate right at the very back of your throat." I push myself in deeper so she takes nearly all of me— nearly, I said, not all, because I'm hung like a stallion—and I let my scalding seed flood her eager throat. "Swallow every drop," I command, my hooded eyes closing as my climax shoots out. Fuck, this feels amazing. The blindfold on her has her clutching my ass to balance herself. Her nails dig into my flesh, as my orgasm pounds powerfully right through my dick like an avalanche. I'm coming hard but I'll want more after this. I always do with her. I crave her tight cunt . . . her tight, innocent little cunt that I've corrupted, that I've turned into a greedy little harlot that needs me, and only me, to function properly.

I am Finn.

And the one thing I've learned is:

I'm every woman's fucking fantasy.

"Get up, baby. Steady now, I've got you." She stands up slowly, swallowing the last drop, using my hips as her guide, walking her hands around my waist. Her breasts have gotten bigger because of all the attention I've been lavishing on them lately, her pussy more swollen. She's ravenous for me. I've had her on a diet. A fuck diet. I want her screaming my name, begging for it.

I'm her drug.

"Bend down," I say. I lay my hand on the small of her back as she hairpins her lithe body forward. My gaze focuses on her sweet ass, and I toss up the different possibilities in my mind. Today I'll fuck her, good and hard. That's what she craves. "Good girl. Touch your toes." She does as bid, and when her hands reach the floor, her dripping wet pussy is on full display. "Tell me what you want."

"I want you to fuck me."

"What's the magic word?"

"Sir. I want you to fuck me, Sir."

"What else?"

"I've been a bad girl. I need you to spank me."

My eyes set alight, glinting in the semi-darkness like a fox eyeing up his juicy meal. Her ass like a peach, her swollen center like a split fig, pink and lush on the outside, fresh and tight in the middle. My left palm comes down hard on her left cheek, my right hand a sting to her right. She cries out, but not in pain. With yearning.

"Please, Sir, fuck me."

"Watch your mouth," I rumble, striking that now rosy ass again. But as soon as the sting of the spank has rung through the room, I bend down and swoop my tongue over her wound, let it ride along her crack and lap up her quivering slit. Fuck, she's wet. My cock expands at her carnal desire. She's balancing her hands flat on the floor the way I've trained her so I can slam her from behind. The huge head of my cock teases her opening, in wait for the right moment to strike. This is the part that drives her wild with anticipation, the moment that has her begging.

"Please!"

"Please, what?"

"Please shove it in."

"Watch your dirty mouth spouting crass verbs

like that."

I hold her ass with one hand and with the other I smear my pre-cum, which is oozing out of the wide crest of my cock, all around her engorged clit. I slap her nub with my dick, making her moan, then bring my arms around her breasts. I'm so hard it needs no guidance as it prods in and out, just enough to keep her begging, while I play with her nipples, twisting them, tweaking them, kneading them (needing them) between my forefinger and thumb.

"Please!"

I slam into her all the way—deep—and she cries out, screaming my name. Not Sir, but Finn.

"This. Is. Mine," I rumble. I'm pumping her ruthlessly, but she loves it. So much, I can feel her orgasm tighten and clench around my erection, its ardor so electrifying I come once more, bursting inside her beautiful body.

Yes, I'm her Dom.

But the irony is . . .

She's got all the control, because I've fucking well fallen in love.

"HE'S HAD A WET DREAM AGAIN." The

nurse titters with amusement, waking me up with her giggles.

Another nurse, with a voice I don't recognize, adds, "Have you ever seen a patient with such a huge schlong?"

"Ssh, clean him up quick, Dr. Jürgen's coming."

12

Janie.

MY CELL BUZZED me out of a deep sleep. I had forgotten where I was and then, after I cracked open an eye, remembered I was in a hotel. In Vegas.

I grabbed my phone. "Hello."

"Janie, it's Elodie."

"Thank God. How's Daniel?"

"He hasn't woken up yet."

My pulse began to race. "Oh, no!"

"The doctors say that the induced coma was a good thing, that Kristin behaved ethically, that she did everything right."

"But that's crap, he . . . he woke—"

"They're saying that's unlikely and there is nothing to that effect in his medical notes . . . are you sure you didn't imagine it, Janie? That he woke from his coma that time?"

I could hardly believe my ears. "Not you, too?"

"Look, I'm on your side, and even if Kristin Jürgen did the right thing by Daniel, she's still a monster in my eyes. I'm just saying, that *profession-ally*, nobody can fault her as a doctor."

That figures . . . the award winning doctor of the month, posing as fucking Florence Nightingale!

My nails were digging so hard into my palms they were almost bleeding. I was beyond tense and furious. I tried not to lose it completely. "What about the marriage stuff?" I shot out.

"She says she doesn't know what you're talking about, that you've been imagining things. That she never pretended she was married to Daniel. She laughed about it, saying what a wild imagination you have."

"She's insane! Did you speak to the concierge at Daniel's hotel? Ethan?"

"Yes, he says it was your choice to leave Daniel's hotel, that you shot out of there all of a sudden, and that he doesn't know anything about

Kristin Jürgen claiming she's married to Daniel."

"This is crazy!" I screeched. "I feel like I've walked onto the set of a Hitchcock movie. The woman is insane!" I wondered what Kristen's agenda had been, pretending she was Daniel's wife. Obviously her plan had been to forge a marriage, wanted to prepare everyone (namely me) for it, and then, because of Sophie's fancy doctors getting involved and stopping his coma in its tracks, wasn't able to see it through. Marriage to Daniel would have made her a very rich woman. Beyond rich. And with him in a coma, or worse, dead, she could have funded her sick experiments to her heart's content. As I was sifting this all through my shell-shocked mind, I remembered the most urgent thing of all: "Anyway, more importantly, will Daniel be *okay*?"

"Nobody knows yet. He still hasn't come out of his coma. They think maybe another twenty-four hours. He's under observation."

"Will he be *okay*?" I realized I'd just asked that question. "What if that bitch gets to him again?"

"Stay calm, Janie. Like I said, he's under observation. One of our doctors is sticking around until he's awake. And his mom is here from Switzerland. She's given the green light for him to be transferred. To a hospital in LA, when he comes to . . . whenever he's ready."

"But meanwhile that lunatic is hovering around! She could do anything! Why is your team of doctors on her fucking side? I thought that was the whole point! That you could move mountains, that you could make Kristin Jürgen fucking disappear!"

Elodie was silent. "I agree, I thought they'd be more active . . . more, as you say, 'on our side.' After all, my mom's paying them enough. Shaking off this doctor-sticking-up-for-other-doctor bullshit is more complicated than we thought. They simply refuse to cast any malpractice blame on their colleague Kristin."

"And what about the chimps? Isn't that proof enough she's a monster?"

"No proof."

"WHAT?"

"*We* have clandestine proof, *we* know the lab was hers, but technically, legally—and hey, legally, by the way, we have no leg to stand on because we were breaking into someone else's property without a warrant—Kristin's in the clear. No rent, no ownership, nothing states that the premises are hers."

"What about Remy? We can prove she was paying him to abduct me, and where he took me. Right next *door* to her freaking lab!"

"That's another problem. Remy's gone MIA. He's not picking up his phone. Not at his apartment. Nobody's seen him."

"How do you know his phone number? He never gave it to you." As I said this, I remembered what Elodie's day job was, not to mention the moonlighting. "Crap," I said, "he's *missing*, really?"

"Not looking good."

"Oh my God, I pray he's okay." I was hoping that Remy had hit a bar somewhere, and was simply conked out on someone's couch for the night. My mind wandered to Kristin's other illegal wrongdoings. "What about Natasha's will? You got any news on that? The forgery handwriting experts?"

"Kristin's been given the all clear on that, too. They say the will is genuine."

"*Really*? And these are experts you *trust*?"

"They're supposedly the best."

"Damn, this woman's clever."

"That's what Alessandra says. She still refuses to believe Kristin's innocent."

"And your mom? What does she think?"

"There are some jealousy issues going on. She's accusing Alessandra of having been Natasha's girlfriend and still being in love with her."

"But Natasha's dead! How can she be jealous of a dead woman?" I realized she wasn't the only one jealous of Natasha . . . I'd nursed my fair share of that green-eyed disease also.

"Yup, I know. That's my mom for you. This information's between you and me, by the way, Janie."

"My lips are sealed." I had visions of two un-quenchable flames in a raging lesbian bonfire: hot-bloodied Italian actress Alessandra, and poison dart-eyed Sophie. Plates flying around the room? Smashed furniture? Scary . . .

Elodie exhaled a pent-up breath that spoke of exhaustion and exasperation. "Look, I need to get off the line and locate Remy."

"Good luck, I so hope you find him. Look, my friend Star's here and is keen to help, but I have to get going to the hospital."

"I know Star. I've got her number. I'll call.

Well, good luck to you, too, at the hospital. By the way . . . a warning, just so you know . . . "

Scalding adrenaline pumped like liquid molten into my heart. "What?"

"Daniel's mom? She really likes Kristin. Adored Natasha apparently."

"Didn't she know that Natasha was in love with another man? That her marriage to Daniel was a joke?"

"Nope. His mom thinks that she was the perfect wife for Daniel."

"So basically, in everyone's eyes—except for ours—Kristin Jürgen and Natasha Jürgen are fucking saints?"

"Looks that way."

"So who's there *right now* at the hospital with Daniel?"

"His mom, Kristin, our doctor, Doctor Nadil, and the usual nurses."

"I need to get there immediately."

"Janie, be careful. Don't get yourself kicked out of there. Remember, you are not 'family,' and until Daniel wakes up, it's at their discretion to let you visit."

Silence while I took in Elodie's wake-up-and-smell-the-coffee words. What a mess.

"Look, Janie, I've got to go. Talk to you later."

As I was brushing my teeth, Dad suddenly called, wondering how Daniel was doing. I had to bite my tongue and not let on about the nightmare I was going through. Having him worry about me wouldn't help the situation.

"That accident changed Will," Dad revealed. "But in a good way. It's almost as if he's more focused now. He's applied to do an internship in New York with a stockbroker, or maybe it's a hedge fund manager—something to do with money, anyway."

"Is that a good idea?" I said, knowing that Will had a propensity to become obsessive when he dealt with numbers. I tapped my foot with agitation—right now wasn't the moment to discuss Will's future—I couldn't give it the time or attention it deserved—all I could think about was Daniel.

"You know what?" Dad went on. "I think it is. It could be a real career for him."

I had to hold back my tears. I wanted to burst out crying and tell my father everything. "Dad, I miss you so much."

"Me too, honey."

"I love you."

"I love you too, baby, is everything okay? You're still staying at Daniel's apartment?"

"Yes," I choked, swallowing my lie. "It's all fine . . . I mean, I'm crossing my fingers about Daniel, but I'm okay. Don't worry about me, Dad, I'll be fine. I'd better go. Give Will a big hug from me."

13

Daniel.

"HOW'S THE PATIENT doing?"

The voice is gruff and low. A man. He's new, I haven't heard that voice before.

"I think he's on the mend, Dr. Nadil." *Oh fuck, it's her . . . she's back.*

I can feel his large hands on my pulse. Steady hands of a man I can trust. *Relief at last.* But he mumbles something I can't hear about lowering the dosage . . . his footsteps getting quieter, and then a closing door. Fuck, he's gone. The room is silent for a beat, and then . . .

"Honestly, Bettina, there's no need for Daniel to be transferred to LA. He's in good hands here.

Who better to look after him than family?"

You fucking psycho!

"Oh, Kristin, thank God you've been here for him." *My mother's clueless voice.* Thanks for gracing me with your presence, Mom.

"I know. Poor Daniel. He was in bad shape but I did everything I could, and it looks as if he has a fighting chance now." *Butter wouldn't melt in your fucking mouth, would it, you charlatan . . . how can my mother be such a dimwit?*

"I owe you his life, Kristin, honey. How can I repay you?"

Get out the checkbook, Mom, that's what you usually do, isn't it? Anything to avoid intimacy. Money buying you out of every situation that makes you uneasy.

"You're his mom and you trust me. *That* is payment enough. Being a neurologist is tough. Sometimes—like in Natasha's tragic case—there's nothing you can do. It's heartbreaking. But you know I'll do *anything* for Daniel. I love him like a brother. He and Natasha were so in love, so happy together."

I try to open my mouth to speak. "*Stop with the fucking fantasies!*" But no sound leaves my lips. There are two cloying perfumes circling me now, as if battling for which can be the sickliest, the most repugnant to my olfactory sense.

"Kristin? Kristin? I just saw Daniel twitch, like a grimace—he moved his mouth!"

"Yes, that's normal with coma patients, Bettina, dear. It doesn't mean they're awake, unfortunately."

"I'd love to stay, my dear, until Daniel wakes up properly, but I'm meant to be at an important fundraiser in Hawaii tomorrow. I simply cannot miss it. Everybody who is *anybody* will be there. My jet is scheduled to fly out this afternoon. Kristin, would it be considered very unfeeling if I didn't stay much longer? I mean, he doesn't even know I'm here, so—"

"Of *course* not, Bettina, *I'm* with him. Oh, by the way, I have a special gift for you. Hang on a second, while I find it in my purse."

"A gift? Kristin, *really*, you shouldn't have."

As I lie here, I'm wondering what is coming next. There's a catch. Kristin is up to something. Whenever she used to give Natasha a gift, there was an ulterior motive. *What's she after, I wonder?* She wants something in return, for sure.

"It's antique, Bettina, genuine Art Deco. Open

the box."

"Oh my Lord! Kristin, this choker is . . . I have no words . . . these pearls are simply beautiful! The colors, the tones . . . and look! A diamond clasp! But it must have cost a *fortune*."

"Bettina, you're *family*, no expense spared. Do me a favor, though; wait until you're back in Switzerland before you wear them. You can never be too careful here in the States."

"Of course, my dear, if you think that's best."

"Oh, and one more thing before you rush off, there's something you *can* do for Daniel.

"I can't stay long, my dear, I—"

Ah, here it comes . . . the catch, the trade-off.

"I understand, Bettina, it won't take long. But as you're not able to be here, as next of kin, you can give me power of attorney to oversee anything that needs attention. Then you can rest at ease, knowing how Daniel will be under my expert care. I could call my lawyer to set it up, if you like—he's a close friend of Daniel's, and is only around the corner. He could come right away."

"That's a splendid idea, I hadn't thought of that."

"Oh, and . . . another thing, Bettina, there's

this actress that once did a job with Daniel. She's been stalking him for a couple of years now. He tried everything to keep her away, but she's delusional. Thinks they're in love. Sweet kid, but I'm worried she could be dangerous. I'd like you to forbid her to visit. She's called Janie something-or-other. Dark hair. Big, Bambi-brown eyes. But don't be fooled."

No! I'm groaning. Trapped inside my own mind. I try to sit up, but my brain is a whirl of colors and flashes of light. Not able to make me her husband, Kristin has done the next best thing . . . taking control of me through this fucking power of attorney. I see a bright red truck looming in front of me . . . the visions again. I'm spinning, swirling . . . someone . . . anyone . . . let me out of here before I get run over!

14

Janie.

I RACED TO the hospital, not even bothering to shower or have breakfast. But before I had even gotten to Daniel's room, I was stopped by a burly male nurse.

"Are you Janie Cole?" he asked.

"Yes." The second I said 'yes' I was aware I'd made a grave mistake. Duh.

"Sorry, no visitors for Mr. Glass, right now."

"No visitors, or is it that just *me* you don't want visiting?"

"I'm sorry, the patient is in no condition to see anyone, he's—"

"Has he awoken from his coma?"

"I'm not at liberty to divulge—"

"Please!" I yelled. "Can't you just give me that? Tell me he's okay?" My eyes were brimming with tears, heat rushing to my face in a flaring rage.

"Yes," the nurse conceded, his expression a little kinder now, although he stepped his large frame into my personal space, so I was forced to retreat. "He is stable, but Miss, I'm sorry, you cannot enter." He crossed his hairy arms with deliberation. A human barricade.

"He'll want to see me. Ask him. Ask him if he wants to see me! Daniel?" I shouted out. "Daniel, can you hear me in there?"

The nurse laid his hands on my shoulders and pushed me away from the door. "He's awake but not aware. I'm afraid Mr. Glass is not in a fit state to make decisions right now. Please leave, Miss, before I call security."

I stomped off, my ears hot with fury. I needed to get something to eat, my stomach rumbling with hunger, my head dizzy. I'd been neglectful with my supplements—obviously hadn't had them at hand while I was locked up, and had stupidly forgotten to take them last night with my meal. I called Elodie, wondering if Kristin had stabbed

Daniel with yet another syringe to make him go gaga, or if he really was "unaware," and just needed time to come to.

"What's Sophie's number?" I asked Elodie, without even saying hello. "I need to get the okay from the neurologist she procured so I can be allowed to visit Daniel."

I could hear a long sigh coming down the line. "I'm so sorry, Janie, I was about to call you. Dr. Nadil's been called away on an emergency. Some senator's son has been in a car crash and the family has summoned him. He's a close friend, apparently. He said he felt completely assured that Daniel was okay, and that Dr. Jürgen had behaved in a very professional manner. He refuses to stick around, even though he was offered silly money by my mother to stay."

"So this whole thing has been a waste of energy, money, and time?"

"No, not at all. Daniel's alive, isn't he? He's stable. Things could be so much worse. And all this will be noted in his medical file now, having been overseen by a third party: Dr. Nadil. We just need to find a safe way to get Daniel out of there as soon as possible."

I leaned against the wall to steady myself. Every time we seemed to be making progress another jagged obstacle was thrown in our path. I wondered how much more I could take of this. "Where's your mom?" I spat out, secretly blaming Sophie for all this, although logically I knew it wasn't her fault; she'd tried her best, she really had.

"She left for Paris. I'm sorry, Janie, but this whole Natasha Jürgen thing has opened up a can of worms between her and her wife. Maman says she's done all she can for Daniel. Not that she doesn't care about him, but her focus was, and still is, on Alessandra and the animals. I feel badly for you, but the 'rescue mission avenue' has been exhausted, we can't rely on my mom for anything more. We need to work out something ourselves. I have money, but I'm not sure what good that will do at this point. The medical world is very cliquey, very protected."

"You need to get in to see him, Elodie. They won't let me, I was barred from entering his room."

"Um, not so simple."

"What do you mean?"

"My mom had a big argument with Dr. Nadil,

112

right in front of Kristin. Kristin got wind of the whole thing, and although she's all smiles with Dr. Nadil—she has to be because he's so respected—she doesn't want me, or anyone connected with us, hanging around. She worked out pretty fast that me and my nurse's uniform were bogus."

"But she doesn't get to tell everyone what to do! She isn't Daniel's wife like she was pretending."

"I'm afraid she does."

Fear rushed to my veins again—had they discovered she'd married Daniel, after all? "Does what?"

"Does get to boss everyone around," Elodie said. "At least till he's conscious and can make his own decisions. Daniel's mom Bettina was here yesterday. They drew up papers with a lawyer. Bettina, as next of kin, gave Kristin power of attorney."

I felt that familiar, watery feeling in my knees again. I could sense them giving way as I swayed, then tumbled to the floor.

15

Daniel.

I AM SWIMMING up from a deep sleep, higher and higher, my arms pushing the water as I come up to catch my breath. I can see the waves above my head and light from the sky overhead. But it's out of focus. I try to keep my eyes open, but the pressure on my head is immense. I close them again. There, that's better.

"Daniel, don't flinch, please. I need to attach these electrodes to your head and I can't when you *move* like that! It's three a.m., and I've got you all to myself for a few hours, so *please* cooperate, why can't you make this easy for me, goddammit!"

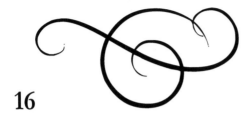

16

Janie.

THE LIGHTS WERE bright, blinding my vision even though my eyes were squeezed shut. I could hear all kinds of different voices surrounding me, helicoptering above me. I tried to open my lids but my weary body wouldn't allow me. At last I cracked open an eye and recognized the familiar surroundings. I was in a bed. My arm felt pinched and I saw a tube attached. A drip. Starchy white sheets. The smell of disinfectant. I made out a woman in uniform in my peripheral vision, leaning over me: a nurse.

Then I recalled blacking out earlier, here at the hospital, after I'd tried in vain to see Daniel.

I took in a long breath through my nose. A scent I recognized from somewhere—where? A sweet, heavy, woman's perfume.

And something told me I was done for.

As good as dead.

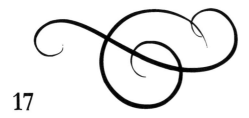

17

Daniel.

THE PAIN IS unbearable as if my skull is in a vice being tightened by the second. It's dark, the lights are off—there are no creaks of light filtering through my closed eyes. But white flashes are inside my brain like exploding stars—the kind of stars you see when you bash your head on something, only a thousand times worse.

The silence tells me it's the middle of the night. There is only one person here.

My torturer: Kristin.

In my normal life I could have her on the ground in seconds. But what is happening isn't normal, and it sure as hell isn't a life. I have never paid much attention to God, never felt I needed Him. But right now I'm screaming for His help. Making deals. If He can just stop this pain, I'll do anything in return.

Anything.

I'm offering up all I can think of that may interest Him. Foundations for charity—not that I haven't already been generous over the years—but I'll donate the lot. Hand over my fortune.

I ask two things in return. To get this agony to stop and to have Janie by my side.

I hear a noise. At first I think it's within my head, but then I'm aware of voices. The pain abruptly stops.

Has He answered my pleas?

"Whatever you're doing, cut it out," a woman's voice commands. "Take that shit off his head, turn off the power, this second. Star has you on film, Kristin. For the last few minutes we've been recording your every move."

Few minutes? Fuck, why didn't they stop her sooner? Did she say 'Star?' Do I know that voice? Who is she? The accent's French. I feel a release. My head is free. Light. Thank you, thank you, Whoever you are Up There, you've got my vote from now on.

Kristin lets rip a throaty cackle. I'd know that laugh anywhere—just like her sister's. "All I was doing was measuring Daniel's dreams. It's an EEG scan. It doesn't hurt him. Honestly, this is normal practice, nothing to be worried about."

"Tell that to my ten million Twitter followers," says Star, confirming to me that it is, in fact, Star Davis. *Where the hell did she pop up from?*

"Kristin, you'll do exactly what we tell you, from now on," the French girl says. "You want this live on *YouTube* for the whole world to see? Daniel's pretty damn popular with the ladies—he's quite a celebrity. You think they want to see him being tortured like one of your lab animals?"

Another nervous laugh from Kristin. "How do you know about . . . it was *you?* You broke into my laboratory? Look, I don't know who the hell you are, but I'm a respected doctor and researcher. And you can't prove a thing. In the eyes of the medical board and my peers, I have done nothing wrong. I'm calling security *right now*, you'll be sorr—"

"Not so fast, you fucking bitch." There's a scuffle . . . a loud thump that sounds like someone falling with a crash to the floor . . . then silence.

Muffled whispers. The door opens.

"Are you done?" *Jesus, it's my nurse. She's in on this too?* "Oh, God, what have you done to Dr. Jürgen?" she cries. "I'll lose my job!"

"Just giving her a taste of her own medicine, Dexter style," Star says. "She'll be fine in an hour. She'll wake up a bit groggy, but she's okay. Just an injection of barbiturates. Let's get her on one of these beds, and wheel her over to another wing. Here, help me lift her up. Fuck, she's heavier than she looks."

"I-I-," my nurse stutters, "I had no idea you'd knock her out, I—"

"Relax, remember what I promised you? A night with me and Jake at the Oscars? You'll forget all about this little incident when I have you dressed in Armani and coming with us to the Vanity Fair after-party. You play dumb, remember? Just like we discussed. You were visiting the ladies room at the wrong moment, that's all. You have no idea what happened. One minute Dr. Jürgen was here with Daniel, the next she wasn't. You'll be fine, believe me. Just stay cool."

"I'd love to finish the bitch off right here, right now," the French girl hisses, "but that would cause too much suspicion. I'll get her one day though. Revenge is a dish best served cold."

I tumble that phase over and over in my mind . . . *Revenge is a dish best served cold*. I'm thanking the Man in the Sky . . . or the Woman? *Thank you for stopping the pain*. All I want now is to see Janie.

But before I know it I, and everything around me, fades to black.

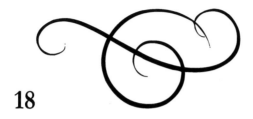

18

Janie.

IT'S BEEN A week since Kristin was finally stopped in her tracks, thanks to Star and Elodie.

I was fine after twenty-four hours or so. It took Daniel a while to be *compos mentis*—for the drugs to be flushed totally out of his system, but slowly he emerged. He told me that he'd had vivid dreams, mostly concerning visions of pink elephants, a brief visit from his mother, and his dead father, and Natasha, who apparently "forgave" him. Oh yes, and that his character Finn from *The Dark Edge of Love* had made a few appearances. Other than that, he didn't remember a thing. Zilch.

Thank God. I held off revealing the truth. I wanted him to fully recover, not be fuelled by rage and end up back in a coma from a heart attack.

His main concern, of course, was not for himself, but for me, having relapsed into my anemic state for not taking care of myself properly. He couldn't understand why I'd missed meals, hadn't taken my supplements, to the foolish extent of ending up in a hospital bed again. "Silly girl," he admonished several times. "Silly, silly girl, Finn might have to give you a good spanking." I was desperate to explain what had happened, but I didn't want him losing it, which he would have done if he'd found out the truth about Kristin.

Besides . . . Elodie—with her skills at hacking—had Kristin's every move monitored. She told her that if she continued to practice medicine, or have anything at all to do with the medical world, she'd expose her. Despite Kristin's insistence that she had been innocent and done no harm to Daniel, she obviously didn't want to take any risks. Far better, Elodie explained to her, to resign from her job, use the generous inheritance from Natasha, and keep quietly to herself. If Kristin went near an animal again, Elodie warned, she'd let the world know what a monster she was. Elodie had tabs on her computer, her banks, her social life. Kristin would be hard-pressed to make the wrong move.

All this while we waited for Daniel to return to his old self. Then we'd see what the consensus was . . . expose Kristin or not? It was a tough call. I had never been one for revenge or "an eye for an eye," but Elodie, Alessandra, and Sophie felt differently. Star wanted her fully exposed, her little film at the ready. Sophie actually thought it would be easier to have Kristin "topped off," and Elodie even offered to do it, although that part they kept silent from Star.

"Too much hassle," Elodie had said, "keeping an eye on Kristin long term. What, am I supposed to spend my whole life keeping tabs on the bitch? A nice, clean shot to the head would be the most humane way for her to go." Remy, who had reemerged (after a drunken night on the town that time he vanished), was keen to be Elodie's "right hand man." He'd been trailing around after her, love-struck as a puppy. Bonnie and Clyde in the making?

Then Sophie changed her mind and decided

Kristin didn't deserve humane treatment, and thought she would be better off served with her own medicine (ha ha), locked in a cage with electrodes screwed to her head, or dropped by helicopter into the middle of a remote rainforest with chimps and gorillas to do what they wanted with her. I kept out of the discussion, but agreed that the biggest punishment of all would be for the world to know who she truly was.

"Don't be so sure," Alessandra had warned. "There's a whole camp out there who'd come to her defense. She'd garner fans worldwide, especially in the medical world. It could backfire."

When Daniel was better, I decided, we'd put it to him and see what his opinion would be. Meanwhile, the three of them: Sophie, Elodie, and Alessandra—like Macbeth's witches brewing their potion in a bubbling cauldron—waited with baited breath for Daniel to recuperate before revealing the full story to him, and promised to hold off exposing Kristin, or doing anything crazy, until he was a hundred percent better.

19

Janie.

W E'D GOTTEN THROUGH an obstacle course, Daniel and I. And miraculously survived. It was almost as if Someone Up There was testing us. To see if we were strong enough, tough enough to endure our ordeal. I hadn't let on to him quite how badly his coma had affected me. We needed to turn the page, move forward.

"We need to get back to work, start rehearsals for *The Dark Edge of Love*. I'm going crazy twiddling my thumbs," Daniel said, stroking my hair as we lay on the bed, a silver tray of half eaten breakfast beside us, he casually reading *The New York Times*. He looked as handsome as ever, a dark lock of his hair flopping over one eye, his cut jaw and cheekbones a testament to his beautiful bone structure, his lips sculpted like they belonged to one of the romantic poets of the last century . . . yet his searing blue eyes looked tired. Worn.

"Drink your juice, finish your eggs and croissant," he said, his bossy tone music to my ears. At least I knew he was on the way to recovery. I bit into my croissant and chewed. Daniel shooed some loose flakes away from my lips. "I'm going to be watching you, making sure you eat properly," he warned. "Plenty of protein and lots of iron-rich greens."

We were back in L.A., where Daniel had been transferred by helicopter to another hospital as soon as he was out of danger. He was one week out of the new hospital and now recuperating at Shutters On The Beach, a beautiful oceanfront hotel in Santa Monica—an iconic "beach house," laid back, but luxurious. I too was resting up, gathering back my strength. His whole coma ordeal was "a blank," he'd told me—he couldn't remember a thing. Thank God. The doctors had made it very clear that he was in no way to get upset or angry, that it could set him back and actually threaten his life. "His heartbeat needs to stay steady," they had warned, "his blood pressure stable. Do *not* let him exert himself or become overly emotional."

So we were both taking it easy; long walks on the beach, holding hands, reading novels, and enjoying the pure pleasure of being together around the clock, hanging out and getting to know each other more. Silly things like *What's your favorite color? Animal? What dead person would you bring back to life and have dinner with?* Questions that seemed childish and insignificant when we'd had a theatre production to do, or a movie to discuss, but things I'd longed to know when he was in his coma.

I drained the rest of my juice then lay my head on his shoulder. I knew he was secretly loving the slow pace of us just being together and doing nothing, but his work ethic was too ingrained to allow him to totally relax.

"You've been out of the hospital five minutes, you're not ready for work," I pointed out, alluding to his comment earlier about 'twiddling his thumbs.' I imagined how frustrated Daniel felt, but the idea of his health being set back because of too much strenuous activity made my stomach fold in on itself. I gave him a warning look.

"It's been an entire week, Janie. We have a film to make. My father didn't raise me to be a slacker."

"So finding out we both love blue, and cats and dogs is 'slacking?'"

A lopsided smile lifted the corner of his mouth. "You don't get to choose cats *and* dogs, I told you already, you have to decide between the two."

"I can't."

He brushed a lock of my hair away from my eye. "Then you're not playing the game properly. Just one, Janie."

"All right, cats, but it doesn't mean I don't love dogs any less."

He winked at me.

"And you, you promised you'd get back to me about your dinner date choice," I said.

He narrowed his eyes. "I'm still mulling it over. This is a once in a lifetime dinner, right? I'd better pick someone with whom I could have a scintillating conversation."

"Einstein."

"Too obvious. Too cliché."

I laughed. It was true, Daniel liked being contrary, favored the obscure. I nestled my head further down his wide chest, relishing the sound of his heartbeat, soaking in the rumble of his deep, reverberating voice, making me remember that he'd been an actor before a director.

He said, "You're still having dinner with Marilyn, then? Really? You don't want to change your mind? *Marilyn Monroe?* Why choose her?

"Because she was everything I'm not. A siren. A blonde bombshell. The sexiest woman who ever lived."

"*You're* the sexiest woman who ever lived," he corrected. I grinned. He made a face. "Marilyn? Seriously? What about Joan of Arc, Queen Elizabeth, or Cleopatra? Or your favorite, Emily Dickinson?"

"Don't judge me. I'd ask Marilyn about the Kennedys, find out the truth. She was a lot more complex a character than people give her credit for, you know," I retorted. "A good actress, too, a great comedian, and she worked her ass off. I'd get a few makeup tips from her while I was at it."

"You don't need makeup, and I prefer your hard-working ass any day, Janie Juilliard." He gave my butt a little squeeze and I was secretly on cloud nine knowing that, in Daniel's eyes, I was more special than Marilyn Monroe.

"But you're right. Scrap Marilyn, I'd have dinner with my mom. Tell her how much I love her. How badly I miss her." I blinked away a pending tear.

Daniel kissed my nose.

"So not Einstein, who then?" I said, veering away from the topic of my mother. Daniel had been driving me crazy for two days with this dinner date thing.

"Still thinking."

"Daniel, that's not fair! Am I going to go to my grave not knowing who your dinner date is?" I playfully bit one of his pecs, or tried to, but it was hard to sink my teeth into such a solid mass of muscle.

He chuckled.

"It's not funny! You're like a fathomless ocean. I never know what's going on inside your head. Why can't you be more . . . more basic."

"Oh I'm pretty basic, all right. Give me your hand, you'll see how basic I am." He took my hand in his and placed it over his groin, where his erection was lying patiently in wait. Alert, keen, and hungry.

I shook my head. "But you need to *rest*, not exert yourself too much. Doctors' orders, remember?"

With his other hand he traced his finger up the nape of my neck, setting goosebumps all over my flesh. I could feel my nipples harden involuntarily.

I suspected one of the reasons Daniel wanted to get back to work was to distract himself, release his energy. Since he'd been out of the hospital we hadn't made love. Well, we had "made love," but we hadn't fucked. I didn't want to. Actually, I did—I was desperate for it—but the doctors had also warned me to go easy. I was terrified of Daniel regressing. But I'd been driving him crazy, and he'd been silently obsessing about it.

He guided my hand along his hard length. Over the thin silk fabric of his pajama bottoms. "Please don't torture me anymore, Janie. I'm telling you I'm not going to keel over if we fuck."

"You've got no idea what it was like for me, do you? Watching you wake up and then slip back into your coma."

I hadn't yet told him the real reasons that had happened; the events concerning Kristin. The other doctors were still maintaining that she had acted "impeccably" and were dismayed when she took a long leave of absence, due to "stress." Little did they know the power Elodie wielded over her with her little film—forcing Kristin to keep to herself. Although I feared it could only be a matter of time until she returned. It was true what Alessandra had said. Kristin was a bit of a star in the medical world and had support. A lot of people wouldn't give a damn about the animals in the lab, and would back her up about her "EEG scans" on Daniel that she had claimed were monitoring his dreams. Even I was beginning to wonder if she'd been innocent. Your brain can do that to you: make you doubt yourself, make you wonder if it had all been your imagination all along.

But I had a sneaky suspicion Kristin was simply biding her time, waiting in the wings.

"You're making up stories, baby." Daniel laughed and ran his fingers through my hair. It was if he'd been reading the thoughts pitter-pattering through my mind. "I can't believe that *mid*-coma, I woke up all of a sudden, had a raging hard-on, got the blow-job of the century from you, asked you to marry me, and then regressed back into a coma—"

I broke in, interrupting his raucous chuckle, my voice squeaking with outrage: "It's true, Daniel, I swear, please believe me!"

Even though I was secretly second-guessing myself, I felt as if I'd been punched in the stomach. Daniel was making light of his marriage proposal. As if it never happened. It wasn't the fact that he couldn't remember that pained me so much, but that marriage was obviously something he was not even entertaining. I felt like a child who had been given a toy that was then snatched away. I knew I was being over sensitive; we had only been dating a couple of months. But I'd been in love with him for years and couldn't see my future without him, and all I wished for was that he felt the same way. In my head I'd been his *fiancée*. Now I was just an actress having "an affair" with him. My old fears lodged themselves deep in my gut. Was he just with me because we had a film to make? I couldn't leave his side, and I wouldn't, but I wanted him to commit to me. One hundred percent.

My silent sulk hung in the air like a wind chime on a still day. I edged away from him and got off the bed. I was holding all these secrets from him about Kristin, and it was hurting me. I felt hollow.

"Baby, where are you going, come right back here!" Daniel patted the bed, his laughter now only a ghost of a smile. Maybe he guessed he'd hurt my feelings.

"I want to tell you so much more, but don't want you freaking out," I said, realizing I'd already revealed too much.

"Fuck me, and I'll tell *you* a secret," he said, winking at me. "I can't hold out any longer, baby. You think it's easy for me to see you slinking around in that silky thing you're wearing, with your smooth gamine legs, and your long hair cascading over your pert nipples and—"

"We've done other things," I reminded him. It was true. He'd given me so many powerful orgasms in the last week, I'd lost count. All without penetration. But I was psychologically blocked; giving *him* oral pleasure could only result in one thing: Daniel slipping back into a coma again. The memory was etched in my brain. It was absurd, but every time I started, and he groaned, I found myself screeching on my brakes. It wasn't just doctors' orders I was following, but my own fear, rooted deep inside my subconscious. Plus, now knowing that marriage wasn't on the cards, sex suddenly felt recreational, not spiritual. I wasn't mentally strong enough for that. Maybe I was subconsciously doing an Anne Boleyn on him; not giving him what he desired until he asked for my hand. Driving him crazy until I got what I wanted. Could I be *that* controlling? Perhaps. But my logic told me that had nothing to do with it. The doctors had advised me to keep him steady, and the way Daniel fucked was anything but . . .

"I need to be inside you, baby. Please. Has there been someone else? Is that your little secret?"

I rolled my eyes like a child. "Don't be ridiculous."

"I was joking." He ran his tongue along his bottom lip then caught that sexy lip lightly with his teeth. "Lie next to me. Come."

I skulked back to the bed and lay beside him, pouting, still fixated on his comment about my imagining his proposal. He wrapped an arm around my shoulder and drew me in close. I could smell him . . . the full-on Daniel Glass aroma, no longer tinged with the odor of the hospital. I inhaled him deeply and it calmed me despite my hurt.

He brought his lips to my ear. "Thinking about your wet, tight pussy has me constantly hard. All I can concentrate on, twenty-four seven, is being deep inside you, fucking you, making you come, and fucking you again."

I wanted more than just sex. I wanted the whole package—and not just the package below his waist. "Daniel, the doctors—"

"Fuck the doctors, I need you, Janie. Look, feel this, feel how hard I still am. You do this. Just being in the same room as you has been driving me insane." He took my hand and placed it once more on his pajama bottoms, where his erection was still thick and eager. I gasped but this time he wasn't going to take no for an answer. He began to undo the ties to his pants and guided my hand under the fabric. My gaze wandered to his chiseled six-pack, which had become even more defined while he was bedridden. He took my thumb and lay it on the tip of his wide, lubricated crest. It was throbbing, moving of its own accord. I felt familiar liquid heat between my thighs.

"Today is the day I'm going to fuck you," he

said, his voice gruff. "No more procrastinating, Janie."

"But Daniel, I'm not ready—"

"You will be, believe me. In a few minutes you'll be lying on your back, legs akimbo, begging me. All those silly excuses about doctor's orders will be out the window, guaranteed."

"They're not excuses . . ." I trailed off, not sure what to say next.

"I know what the real issue is," he said, planting a kiss on my forehead and fumbling in his pajama pocket for what I assumed was a condom.

"What?" Maybe it was true. Maybe the doctor thing was a way of protecting myself from getting hurt. After all the shit I'd been through in the last week: Daniel's coma, being abducted and locked up by Kristin, the animals in the lab, ending up in hospital myself, ill yet again . . . I was more vulnerable than ever, edgy and fearful. I needed to guard myself emotionally.

"Bring your fingers down here," he said, bringing my attention back to his body, guiding my hands under his, between the space of his massive penis and his abdomen. "Do you feel it?"

I giggled uneasily. "How could I not? It's ginormous!"

"Maybe you'll realize, Janie, that what comes attached is something romantic and forever binding, not just sexual."

I was flummoxed, but then I understood what he was talking about. My fingertips felt something hard lodged at the base . . . I stuck my finger through a metal hole . . . a ring?

"A ring?" I asked.

"Not just any ring, baby. Put it on your engagement finger."

I drew my hand out, and with my other hand slipped the jeweled ring onto the fourth finger on my left hand.

He had planned this! My faith in Daniel instantly renewed, my heart beat a million miles an hour. "How did you know the size of my finger? When did you have time to buy this?"

"I bought the ring that very morning. Before the accident. Before your brother Will sent me flying. I've been waiting for the right moment. I know I should have asked you days ago, but I was worried you might say no, and I've been so blissful with you all week, I didn't want to cut my happiness short."

I looked at my hand, but tears were blurring my vision. *As if I would have said no, the silly man!* Didn't he *get* it? Didn't he *know* by now, with every single cell in his body, how deliriously in love I was with him? This was my dream, my fantasy—well, not with Daniel's huge great erection in the marriage proposal mix—that I hadn't envisioned—but this was everything I wanted. To be Daniel Glass's wife and for the whole world to know. He'd bought the ring before his accident! He had wanted to marry me *all along!*

He said, "Not the most conventional place to find your engagement ring, but I wanted to surprise you, and I got the feeling you were running out of patience. I'm going to get down on my knees now, to prove to you I mean it. Down on my knees, and down on you."

I laughed at his joke as he got off the bed and pushed my legs apart, pulling them down so my butt was on the edge of the mattress, my knees dangling over. He shoved his head into the apex of my thighs.

He wasn't kidding. Talk about taking me by surprise. This sex-craving maniac was a true romantic, after all. He'd had me fooled, though.

"You want it, Janie, don't deny it . . . your pussy's glistening like that diamond on your hand." He swept his tongue along my cleft, resting it on my tingling clit. "Will . . . "

He continued his sweet journey, down to my wet opening. "You . . . "

Then he plunged his tongue inside me and I remembered how much I loved being penetrated by him. "Marry . . . "

I whimpered with pleasure. So many sensations coursed through me: happiness, peace, arousal, relief that he wanted me to be his wife . . . I looked at the ring, blindingly sparkly, a massive, oval diamond cut so finely it reflected prisms of light around the room and on the ceiling.

"Me." Daniel punctuated the last word of his proposal with another sweep of his tongue, coaxing out a little cry of pleasure from me.

But my eyes were so focused on my engagement ring, I didn't reply.

"Well?" he said in a hoarse voice, giving my open thighs a squeeze with his hands, and looking up at me.

"This is the most outrageous and unorthodox proposal in the history of all marriage proposals," I gasped, everything south of my waist on fire. I didn't want to sound haughty but hey, all my life I'd dreamed about a more conventional proposal. Everything had happened so fast and unexpectedly. I guessed this was Daniel's plan; to take me off guard and surprise the hell out of me.

"And?"

"You basically asked my pussy to marry you. I want you to say it to my face." Why I was putting him through this torture I wasn't sure, but the words just tumbled out of my mouth.

Daniel stood up and took me by the shoulders, tilting me up so I was in a sitting position, holding me firmly with his strong warm hands. His pajama pants had slid off his hips, revealing that perfect V, and an erection as large and vertically spired as the Washington Monument. He bent down to my level, his lips inches from mine. His breath danced into my parted mouth as I waited for his kiss. He paused, looked intently into my eyes, his gaze serious and fixed. The intense, no-nonsense Daniel Glass that I had fallen in love with when he was my director, bossing me around, telling me what to do.

"Marry me, Janie Cole. Be my wife."

"Is that a question or a command?" I teased.

"It's a command, and by God you'd better obey." I detected a tiny smirk as the corners of his mouth lifted sardonically, before he pressed his lips on mine and drew a kiss from me. I was still dumbfounded—a proposal was the last thing I expected this morning.

But then he pulled his head back and murmured into my mouth, "Answer me, goddamn it, Janie, I'm not fooling around here."

"Y-Yes," I stuttered. "I'll . . . I'll marry you."

"You're sure?" His warm breath came fast.

"Yes, I'm sure."

"You'll be unequivocally mine?"

"Totally, utterly, and completely."

He narrowed his eyes but looked pleased with my answer. "I fucking love you," he said, cupping a hand behind my head, bringing me closer to ensure our lips were touching. I heard a low rasp of pleasure from his throat, letting me know his approval. I let my hands wander down the sides of his muscular body and over his slim hips, one hand gently brushing across his massive, yet silky-soft cock that I was now more than ready for. He was right; I couldn't wait. There was something savagely beautiful about that, knowing how his huge tool could hurt me if he wasn't gentle, yet longing for exactly that; to be ripped open and mercilessly fucked. The whole center of my body was aching for him, pounding with longing, the wetness between my legs evidence of my arousal. A marriage proposal can do that to a girl.

The package was now complete. In every respect.

Inhaling deep through my nose to prepare myself for the kiss of all kisses, I parted my mouth again, letting out a soft mewl as I did so, welcoming Daniel's deft tongue, which he licked seductively along my bottom lip. I moaned with anticipation at the idea of being claimed. Finally, after a week of slow torture for both of us.

I brushed the tip of my tongue lightly against his, and a spasm of hot desire shot directly at my clit like an arrow—just that alone did it, just the tip of his tongue had me melting. My nipples were pebbled, also aching for attention. Every nerve on my body wanted Daniel, and by the sounds of his groans, he hungered for me just as badly. Our tongues then began their dance, clashing together, licking, sucking, plunging, Daniel holding my head in place as if I were a breakable object that he couldn't let go of, his fingers sliding into my hair, caressing my scalp, his guttural groans filling my greedy mouth.

Suddenly, he let go, pulled me up, and lifted me into a standing position. He went down on his knees. I knew what he wanted: for my crotch to be at his eye level—or rather, mouth level.

"No, Daniel, it's my turn. Stand up." I dropped to my knees, his erection resting hard against his navel, his "happy trail"—that fine, soft hair a feast for my eyes. I never tired of observing Daniel. Naked or clothed, he was a specimen of genuine beauty. He wasn't aware of it, though, and didn't even care, had more important things to ponder over than himself. That's what made him even more attractive; there was no arrogance on his part concerning his looks—he wore his beauty with such incidental ease. Like his vintage Patek Phillippe watch—passed down to him from previous generations, wickedly expensive and exclusive, yet something he possessed with nonchalance. A birthright he didn't even acknowledge ... I guessed that sort of casual entitlement held its own brand of arrogance.

He stood up. I grabbed his lean, muscular thighs, my hands were claws as I gripped him tight. His cock was flexing with anticipation.

"Oh fuck, Janie, you'll be the undoing of me."

I wanted him to come in my mouth for a multitude of reasons, mainly to unblock that fear which had been holding me hostage all week: that Daniel would fall back into a coma if I gave him oral sex. But I also knew that he'd been suffering from a case of blue-balls and that he'd need to come several times before feeling sated. Daniel could go for many rounds at the best of times, but now his cock was burning up, the biggest and thickest I'd ever seen it. If I hadn't been so in love with him, I would have found it intimidating.

I gripped his throbbing rod in my grasp, squeezing it at the root, but because of his six foot three frame, I was too low for him to get my mouth around his crest from above. So I darted out my tongue, flicking it at the underside of his balls, sweeping my tongue up and down and around.

"Ah . . . Janie . . ."

I said nothing but filled my mouth with one whole ball, sucking on it gently as my hand rose and fell along his thick girth of his cock.

"Fuck, you're sexy, this is incredible," he groaned.

I took the other testicle and gave it the same attention, as he flexed his hips back and forth. I knew Daniel . . . as much as he loved this, he wanted to fuck me. *Not so fast.* I hadn't reached my goal yet: to rid myself of my coma paranoia. I got up on my feet and carried on with my mission, guiding his huge length into my mouth, the veins pulsing against my tongue as I licked him up and down in preparation. I wouldn't be able to take all of him in, but I knew I could make him come like a rocket being launched to the moon.

I flicked my gaze up sideways and saw his eyes squeeze shut in concentration and pleasure. "Janie, baby, you always drive me wild with this."

I swirled my tongue around the smooth head of his crown, aware for the first time that this piece of his anatomy—hell, all of it—now belonged to me. I was going to be his wife! If any starlets came near him, I'd have the moral right to fight them off. Daniel Glass was *mine*! My mouth pushed down onto his shaft and I suctioned him in, hollowing my cheeks, my head bobbing up and down as he moaned my name.

"Baby, if you keep this up I'm going to come."

"That's the idea," I mumbled, cock in mouth. I didn't let up, my rhythm getting faster and faster as I pumped him. In one final plunge that I knew would do it, I let his erection jam the back of my throat and almost gagged as a hot burst of semen showered into my welcoming mouth.

"I'm coming so hard, baby. Fuck this is intense." His fingers gripped wildly at my hair, pulling it slightly as his orgasm pulsed through him, his cock thickening by the second. I was totally turned on by the power I had to make him so weak with ecstasy. His guttural moans and hooded eyes told me how far gone he was. A woman likes a man to be strong at all times but ironically wishes to have the power to make him weak. This one split-second moment: to have her man at her mercy. Vulnerable. For him to *surrender* to her.

But—as if Daniel had read my Cleopatra mind—he tilted my head back and pulled my mouth off him. "As much as I loved that," he growled between his teeth, "I have to fuck you. Right now."

Weak? Ha! Not Daniel Glass. His erection was still a mighty sword, ready to conquer me. The only thing my blowjob had done was whet his appetite.

And "wet" mine.

He wanted to be in control again.

"Get on the bed and open your legs," he commanded. "I have a surprise for you."

Another surprise? I did as I was told.

He was my director, after all.

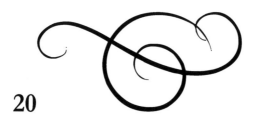

20

Daniel.

MOST MEN WOULD have felt satisfied after being sucked off like that. But I'm not most men. I felt hornier than ever for Janie. She had taken me in her lush hot mouth and made me explode inside, not with just her expertise, but with her whole *Janieness*. She belied herself. Looked innocent, like a petite little virgin, but fuck could she make me come hard. She'd taken care of the beast in me. Now what remained was the animal. I couldn't wait to pound her senseless, fill her up with my thick hard cock. Poor sod had been on sabbatical way too long—all through the coma, and for the past tortuous week. He needed some exercise.

I needed to be inside her. And she needed me inside her.

"Get on the bed and open your legs," I demanded in a rough voice, my dick pulsing with anticipation. I was still as hard as a rock even after having come like the Niagara Falls right to the back of her throat. A little flashback of her a moment ago, sucking me as if her life depended on it, made my cock flex again. I should have been behaving in a more romantic way—I'd just asked her to marry me for fuck's sake—but my carnal need was so overpowering, I couldn't be polite. All I wanted was her hot tight little cunt clenched around me as I pumped her hard. Asking her to marry me had been partly selfish: one of the reasons was so I'd have her in my bed every, single night. No theater touring for Janie from now on, nor making a movie without *me*, right there, on set. She didn't know it yet, but as far as I was concerned, she was all mine.

And I wasn't about to do a timeshare.

I'm not a man who fucks around, I'm by nature monogamous. But once I get started, I can't stop. Janie had switched on my engine.

She lay back on the bed and opened her legs. I grazed my tongue along my top lip, my heart and cock pounding with unprecedented desire. I held my weighty, anxious piece of equipment in one hand, my gaze flicking down for a second to see a droplet of pre-cum on its horny head. No woman had ever gotten me this worked up. Natasha was beautiful, a total siren, but Janie had me doing cartwheels for her. And my cock was always at the ready with Janie—all she had to do was look at me with her big eyes, and that was it—it drove me wild. Her mind, her body, her soul—I wanted all of it and wasn't able to explain why. My love for Janie felt unfathomable, almost painful it was so deep. She was fiercely loyal, had been by my side all through the coma, though she refused to go into details—insisted I wasn't strong enough to talk about it. Whatever, I was happy just to have her at my side. The rest could wait. This loyalty of hers was truly an aphrodisiac. After all the crap I'd gone through with Natasha, having a special woman like Janie so crazy for me was a true gift, and one I didn't take lightly.

But after that beautiful blowjob, she'd woken the sleeping bear. And he was growling for more honey.

No, *roaring* for more honey.

"By the way," I told her, "I have a surprise for you."

She widened her pretty eyes. "As long as you don't relapse, I'm up for a surprise."

My eyes trailed down to Janie's pretty pink pussy, all wet and waiting, plush and soft. I'd asked her the other day how it got to be so smooth and she'd said something about a Brazilian. At first I balked—she'd fucked a Brazilian while I was in my coma? Then I laughed with relief, remembering what that meant. All the more inviting for me. Nothing hidden, all on display . . . I couldn't wait to get right in there.

But first . . .

"Close your eyes, baby."

"Why?" she asked in a singsong voice, obviously suspicious.

"No questions, just be a good girl and do as your told," I said, only half in jest. I knew that Janie liked being ordered around by me even if she pretended she didn't. That's what had started her crush in the first place. My dominant personality. Actresses fall in love with their directors, all too often. Why? Because they subconsciously love being subjugated even if they scratch and fight like tigers in denial. Now I was about to put that theory to the test.

I grabbed the lined handcuffs from my suitcase—the ones I'd ordered, along with the other toys I'd bought for our "rehearsals" for the film.

"Spread your arms as well, so you're like a starfish."

Janie obliged, her eyes still closed. Then I looked at the bed and laughed. The headboard was a soft, upholstered thing with button tufts. There were no posts to latch the cuffs to. I threw the cuffs back in the case.

"What's so funny?"

"Nothing, just me standing here naked with my great big erection. The male body isn't very graceful, I must say."

Her eyes sprang open and she sat up. She bit her lip lasciviously and raked her gaze to my navel and below. "Grace, maybe not, but Daniel, you've got the most beautiful body I've ever seen in my life. Forget the surprise, we'll do it another time. Come right here, right now, what are you waiting for?"

She looked exquisitely beautiful. I never got enough of that little heart-shaped face, framed by her mane of dark hair. Her pert round breasts— the perfect handful, her rosy nipples peaked and alert. Smooth silky skin, pale as a lily. I felt instantly bad for having wanted to play dirty games when she looked so innocent and fresh-faced. This moment should be about making love, not about wild sex games. I took in a deep breath and exhaled. Fuck, I was an asshole sometimes. I needed to get a grip on my libido and calm the fuck down. But I was truly addicted to her. I stood there, mentally counting to ten, to stop myself from ravishing her like a hungry Viking. I remembered the airplane trip when she had burst out crying. Janie fancied herself as a tough, modern woman, but at heart she was as fragile as glass. And I didn't want to chip her, let alone break her. She'd been ill, and in the hospital, on top of it all. I made up my mind, right there, that I'd go easy even though she aroused the carnal monster in me.

"What's wrong? Janie looked alarmed, her doe eyes wide. She glanced anxiously at her ring as if I were about to change my mind about our marriage and yank it off her finger. *As if.*

"I'm not good enough for you, Janie, that's all. I don't deserve you."

"Stop procrastinating already and come here. I don't know about you, but I want to . . . well, you know exactly what I want, Mr. Glass."

21

Janie.

MR. GLASS. HMM, I'd be *Mrs.* Glass soon. A thrilled shiver shimmied up my spine at the thought of it. *Janie Jessica Glass.* Nice. Although I guessed I'd keep Janie Cole for acting as I'd already made a name for myself. Or maybe Janie Cole-Glass. I'd mull that one over.

I observed Daniel as he stood before me, nude, in all his glory. My God, the man was handsome. Like a Greek god, but even better because Greek gods weren't half as well endowed—at least going by the statues at the Met.

But, by the expression in his eyes, I could tell that he was fearful about hurting me. I lay on the bed, waiting for him like an Italian mobster's wife whose husband is so much more worldly. I truly felt like a virgin. His cock was so huge and hard, and every step he took closer to the bed had my heart beating in an excited fear. Yes, fear. There was something dark about Daniel Glass. A flick of the eye, a twitch of the jaw. I never knew where his mood was going, or coming from, and it frightened me. I held him too much in awe, perhaps, so I had often tried to compensate by being sassy and cocky, nonchalant, as if I weren't head over heels for him. Sex with Daniel was amazing, but it was the closeness I craved, the desire to make him need *me* and nobody else. It was a mental thing, not just physical. Orgasms like the ones he gave me didn't just come from his clever tongue or the way he fucked me so perfectly, knowing when to slow down and when to pound my ass off, when to be gentle or when to be rough. It was more to do with the way that he was so committed and intense, so *in the moment. With* me. Just *me*. There for me, *one hundred percent.* As if he revered me, worshipped my body.

I knew this kind of love and connection was one in a million.

I was one lucky girl.

So lucky I was terrified it would all go away.

He lay beside me on the bed, so we were face to face, chest to chest, and he stared into my eyes with a gaze of such longing, such profundity, as if to say, *You and I are for life, please don't ever let me down.*

"I won't ever let you down." I whispered it like a secret. My mouth on his mouth.

"I know."

"I love you," I said seriously.

"I know."

I was waiting for him to repeat the same words, but he just continued with his quiet perusal of my eyes, my face.

"Do you love me too?" I sounded so childish.

"Love . . . love doesn't even begin to encompass the way I feel about you, Janie. What we have is love and far beyond love."

I could feel his huge erection poised at the base of my entrance. His words send a shot of liquid heat to my core and a bolt of desire to my clit. My brain connected so intrinsically to my organs—knowing he felt that way made me so confident, so extraordinary. And above all, sexy. I wriggled into the perfect position, my hands on his shoulders to anchor myself into target position. His cock flexed and I whimpered. I could sense the soft head enter me just a touch.

"Oh God," I cried out.

"You're so fucking wet."

"Wet for fucking," I joked, instantly regretting what had popped out of my mouth, wishing I hadn't turned this spiritual moment into a crass pun.

I laid my hand on his heart. It was thumping so hard in his chest I momentarily panicked. Doctors' orders: *Keep Daniel calm, don't let him get emotionally excited.*

He started prodding me with his erection, in and out, just a millimeter, his eyes hooded with lust. He was groaning and, by the way he was grimacing, he was obviously forcing himself not to ravage me.

"This is no good, Janie, you'll have to get on top and control the pace. I don't trust myself. Use me. Use me to get yourself off." In one swift movement he had me on top, straddling him. I took his cock in my hand and guided it inside me, groaning with pleasure as I did so.

He murmured, "Fuck, baby, you have no idea how amazing you feel."

He was still only quarter inside me, his thick shaft pushing against every nerve in my soaked walls.

"I'm just going to ride the tip of you," I said, "because you're bigger than I remember and it almost hurts." I rested my lips on his and, as I started moving slowly up and down, all the pain vanished, his erection deep inside, but my clit rubbing up and down his stomach, giving me untold pleasure in two places. Daniel had shown me what a vaginal orgasm was like and it had blown my mind—but both erogenous zones being pleasured at once was the epitome of how good sex could be.

His tongue lashed out at mine, plunging inside my mouth, almost brutally, as if it were taking the place of his cock. He raised his hips but was careful not to slam into me—he didn't need to—I'd taken over. Before long I had most of him inside me, filling me up like an overblown Christmas stocking, as I raised my body up and then slammed back down on him, impaling myself on his beautiful, orgasmic-giving tool.

"Janie." His lusty eyes told me all I needed to know—he was loving it.

I carried on with my rhythm, each stroke massaging all the sweet spots for both of us, my nipples keen as bullets. Daniel grabbed a pillow and shoved it roughly behind his head so he was closer. He pulled me down on him by the shoulders and his mouth and tongue lashed at my breasts. I offered him one nipple and he sucked greedily, sending electric currents to my clit and deep within me. All these erogenous nerve endings connected to each other by the brain.

I cried out.

"That's right, baby, use me, use my dick and make yourself come all around it."

I was screaming now, it felt so incredible and I could hardly believe I'd encompassed the whole of him. I pumped hard as Daniel nibbled my nipple, all the sensations swirling inside me. I could feel the build-up swell and about to burst. I was in anther zone now, concentrating hard on my impending orgasm which, before I knew it, had ripped through me in a tidal wave splitting me in two, and then piecing me back together, just as fast, into one exploding, pumping mass of nerves.

I didn't even need to alert him I was coming. He knew it by my body, my inner muscles clenching him, tightening around his expanding bulk, hard and ardent inside me. He was roaring, shoving his hips roughly at me to meet my thrusts as he growled out his climax like a wild beast, semen shooting right to my womb. His thickness inside me, pulsing to the rhythm of his heart—that heart which had professed its love earlier—had me coming again. My clit rubbed up against his hard stomach and sent tingling waves through every cell in my happy body.

This was the best sex I'd ever had.

And before the overwhelming pleasure had even run its course, I wanted more.

He did too. He rolled me over on my back and fucked me ruthlessly, holding my ankle in one hand as he hooked it around the back of his neck.

"Sweet, hot pussy," he thundered. "This is what I live for, *you* are what I live for. Your body, your being, your soul. I'll never be able to get enough of you, my angel."

I wanted to respond with words, but for some reason I couldn't.

He lingered his lips on my ear. "Janie, my healer, my life." I felt him come again.

We lay there, sated, our bodies pressed together with a gleam of sweat, our hearts pounding out the same drum tune. I didn't want this moment to end and hoped I could store it forever in my memory. When I was ninety, would I recall this bliss?

22

Janie.

WE DECIDED—OR at least Daniel did—
that we would honeymoon and marry all
in one go. Daniel didn't want to invite anyone *at all*
to our wedding, greedy to have me all to himself,
but I drew the line at not having my family there
to celebrate. Will and Dad had been my everything
since Mom died, so Daniel relented. He sent one
of his company's private jets to collect them, and I,
forever the wanna-be conservationist, thought it a
horrible waste and a veritable black carbon foot-
print to have a plane fly halfway across the world
mostly empty, so I called my old therapist who had
helped me a lot after Mom died. We'd become

close since our sessions had ended, freed from professional restraints to become friends outside hours. So Daisy and her little girl Amy hopped on board as well. And now that numbers were increasing, Daniel invited an old cricket friend of his called Jesse, a British man who was some CEO of something important.

Destination? Bora Bora.

I hadn't spoken to Daisy for a while, and when I relayed to her all my latest news about *The Dark Edge of Love*, it turned out that she is Pearl Chevalier's best friend! So the next thing I knew, Pearl and Alexandre were also coming along to our wedding, their kids and nanny in tow. Then Star felt left out ("you said it was just family and now I see the whole world is muzzling in."), so she and Jake and their children also made plans to come.

"Now we have to entertain them all," grumbled Daniel, an eye half open as the morning sunlight streamed into our thatched-roofed bungalow, which sat on stilts on the South Pacific Ocean in this tiny chain of French Polynesian islands. Bora Bora is fringed by a barrier reef of coral, which makes it unique. The air smelled of salt and frangipani and jasmine. A wreath of threaded flowers lay at the bottom of the bed.

"That it will never come again ... is what makes life so sweet?" I said.

"You and your Emily Dickinson," Daniel replied sleepily. He pulled me close, wrapping an arm around my shoulder. Our legs were still tangled together, testament to more lovemaking, all through the night. He seemed more insatiable than ever, and I wondered if I could keep up. I was bruised inside and knew I'd been walking around in my bikini a tad self-consciously, remembering the bulk of what had been between my legs—the force of it, the power. The more sex we had, the more Daniel craved. I'd need to take a sabbatical.

His finger touched my clit, incidentally, imperceptibly, tapping me there so lightly my sore and ravaged center could hardly feel it. "I don't have any more orgasms to give you, Daniel."

He laughed, a light, sleepy laugh, full of irony. "Oh yes you do."

He continued playing with me, stroking me, teasing, one hand languidly pinching my nipple, and the other tracing his finger around my core but not on it. Before I knew it, I was willing him to play with that part of me, but he carried on circling me there, avoiding my hard nub, avoiding the part of me that inexplicably begged for another round. My brain was telling me I'd had enough, that my body couldn't take anymore, that we had guests to think of, a wedding to plan. Okay, the hotel was organizing everything, the flowers, the food et cetera, but still, I had to make choices, needed to decide . . .

"Please," I heard myself groan.

"You see. You want it just as much, baby." But he persisted with his tease.

"I'm sore."

"Good. You can spend the day thinking of me with every step you take."

"You'll be watching me," I joked, quoting a certain song with the same stalkerish lyrics.

"Oh, can't you see, you belong to me," he whispered in smart reply. His tantalizing touch was so light, I wasn't used to the neglect on certain areas of my body. "I'm going to make you come this way, Janie. Without touching any of your vital organs."

I laughed. "I think that's impossible."

"We'll see."

His hand trailed up along my belly, lightly tracing the curves of my breasts. My clit tingled and thrummed as Daniel circled each nipple slowly. He pushed me onto my back, tore the sheet away from my body, and I lay expectantly, soothed by the sound of the gentle ocean breeze, the scent of wafting flowers coming and going intermittently, all the more sensual because of my closed eyes.

"Just relax and concentrate on the sound of the waves," he murmured. "I brought something that will have you begging for more."

My eyes flew open. "What?"

"Ssh, you mustn't look, but you can guess when it's over."

"When what's over?" I asked nervously.

"When you've come."

"You're quite the expert, aren't you?" I said, my voice laced with irony, although I knew that Daniel *was* an expert, but I didn't want him to feel too cocky about it, "cock" being the operative word.

He strode across the room and pulled something from his case. I was so used to seeing him with a massive erection, but I hoped this time he really wouldn't use it on me—my poor body simply couldn't take it.

"Shut those pretty eyes of yours, Janie, and don't peek."

"Don't peak or don't peek?" I joked.

"You'll peak alright, to the peak of the highest mountain."

I let my eyes fall shut and felt my heart speed up. I had no idea what he was planning but had to trust he wouldn't hurt me. I was a bit of a wimp when it came to pain.

"I'm just going to put this blindfold on you, baby. Just to make sure you don't cheat."

"You don't trust me?"

"It'll make the experience more sensual," he assured me, in his late-night, gruff voice. A voice that sounded as if he'd binged on more cigarettes and whiskey than Don Draper, although, funnily enough, Daniel had never smoked in his life and rarely drank.

The blindfold was weighty on my lids but it felt great. I smelled lavender, as well as the frangipani.

"It's stuffed with buckwheat or something to put weight on your eyes—and there's lavender inside also. What do you see?"

"Nothing. Pitch black."

"Good. Just concentrate on the sounds around you. The sound of my breath, the lull of the lapping waves. Think of this as meditation. Clear your mind from general chit-chatty mind-thoughts, judgment, desires or outcomes."

It was true. I had a thousand thoughts swirling in my head. Daniel and his huge cock. My needs, yet how sore I felt inside. Pearl and Alexandre— had their plane landed? Would my simple linen dress be good enough, maybe I should have brought something fancier for my wedding gown. Could I act? What would happen when we got back to work? Was it a fluke that I got nominated for a Tony Award for *Where The Wind Blows*? WHAT IF THEY DISCOVERED I WAS A FRAUD?"

"Relax, Janie," Daniel mumbled in my ear. He stroked my hair, soothing away my over-active ramblings that did me no good at all. "Just empty your mind and think of nothing else than the waves. Just the soft lapping waves, right beneath our bungalow. The turquoise water, clear and clean. The fish swimming beneath us, resplendent, multicolored, and going about their lives with absolute ease."

I thought of sharks, suddenly, and wondered if they'd gobble up the unsuspecting fish, but Daniel had moved on . . .

"The aroma of frangipani . . ." I didn't hear the rest but felt and incredible sensation of something light whispering across my nipples. It circled my breasts, around and around. I could feel my nipples harden and my pussy moisten.

"So beautiful," I heard him say.

I was trying to work out what it was that was teasing me. Something soft. A feather? No. Tassels? It stroked along the center of my torso, down, down, avoiding the cleft of my pussy just by a millimeter. I moaned and rocked my hips up, hoping to meet whatever was giving me this indescribable pleasure. It traveled along my thighs, down my calf to my toe, where it lingered on my foot, ticking the erogenous zone—that pressure point in the middle underside of my sole. My clit was thumping to the rhythm of the strokes, and just when I thought it couldn't get any sexier, Daniel's thumb and forefinger (yes, I knew them by heart) squeezed my left nipple. Pulling, releasing, pulling, releasing. My whole body was throbbing.

I was lost in ecstasy. He tugged at it harder, meanwhile continuing with his "reflexology" treatment that had me squirming in my blindfold, still in total darkness as I was. He was right. I had lost all thoughts of everything, even the sounds around me. All I could do was *feel*. He hadn't even touched me between my legs, not even lightly brushed past my clit, but I was groaning with carnal pleasure. He moved onto my other nipple and the unexpected change, of concentration on my part, caused tingles deep within my groin to explode.

"Oh, Daniel." I felt a rush of blood to my central core as an orgasm ripped through the middle of me. I was fucking the air, gyrating my hips, longing for some contact on my pussy, even though my climax was so full and real. Just then, the same tool Daniel had been using to give me such pleasure rapped at my clit. A shocking sting.

"Horny girls deserve to be punished," he said, the tassels of what I now realized was a whip slashing at my cleft, the sharp pain bringing in another orgasmic wave. "Need to be scolded for being so fucking hot, so fucking tempting. Jezebel . . . Eve with her juicy rosy apple. Making our dicks so hard, making us think of nothing but sex all day long."

I wanted to laugh but couldn't. The whip came down on my breast, making the nipple tweak and more pulsation pound between my legs. Daniel ripped off my blindfold, straddled me without sitting on me, his fist clamped around his enormous cock that he was pumping hard with his hand. He pressed its head on my nipple, his precum sticky and hot, then pushed my tits together with his large hands making a valley for his erection to bury itself in. In the past, this hadn't been possible, but my breasts had grown lately, in fact they were darn right swollen. All the attention? Or was my body telling me something? He started fucking my tits, his groans of pleasure an aphrodisiac, and my orgasm tingled on. Quieter, less intense, but still there, my swollen center a mass of over stimulated nerves, even though Daniel had not fucked me or even touched me there. Just that eager little thrash, nothing too much, but enough to give it the attention it needed.

Having this man I was in love with fuck my tits was one of the sexiest things I'd ever experienced. His devotion to those girls of mine, and my *foot* (crazy, eh?) had given me a mind-blowing orgasm, seconds before Daniel snapped the whip on me, which enhanced every sensation even more. How did he get his timing so right, each and every time?

This was the question on my mind, when his hot, creamy seed detonated all over my boobs and neck.

He growled out, "You see? We don't even need to fuck. One day I'll be able to make you come just with my mind. You and I are one, Janie. Oh, baby, you always make me come so hard."

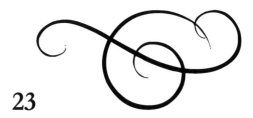

23

Daniel.

I THOUGHT OUR pre-wedding dinner with the "crowd," as I'd nicknamed them, would be exasperating. But it wasn't. Originally I had wanted Janie all to myself for our nuptials, but soon a whole slew of friends and family joined us. At the last moment, I called my mother, but she said she had just gotten back from Hawaii and "wasn't in the mood" for more tropical weather. That sounded about right; her mood took precedence over my wedding. Her loss, not mine. She was missing out not getting to know my fiancée. She never had gotten over Natasha—those two were peas in a pod. Secretly, I was relieved, though. Relieved to not have to entertain her.

Will, and Janie's dad had arrived early that morning. Will mended, except for a slight scar on his cheek that I had apparently given him with a sharp kick. It looked rather becoming, the kind a bygone, black and white movie star might sport in a pulp thriller. Will was beyond apologetic, but of course I couldn't remember a thing. Strange that, to be completely oblivious of a whole chunk of time. I remembered walking into my hotel lobby, and the rest was a blank. The hospital . . . snippets came and went but nothing substantial. I got the feeling that Janie was hiding something from me, though, and when her ex therapist friend Daisy showed up, their voices hushed as soon as I approached them by our plunge pool earlier that day, I knew they had changed the conversation for my benefit, and it made me very curious.

"So are you ready to get back to work?" Alexandre asked me with a hint of a smirk on his face. I guessed he was referring to the subject matter of *The Dark Edge of Love,* and I couldn't deny that the BDSM nature of my role had me itching to rehearse a little more. Playing with the whip that morning had been spontaneous, not planned at all, but Janie had loved it. I could feel myself harden up just recollecting her orgasmic face, her parted mouth, the way she squirmed on her back as I slapped her wet pussy as she screamed out her partly tantric climax. I'd hardly touched her. I concentrated my attention back to Alexandre, glad I was sitting down at the dinner table so he couldn't see the telltale signs of my dirty thoughts.

"Yup, I've been idle for too long," I admitted. "I'm one of those boring workaholic Americans," I jested. "I know you Europeans appreciate a good long lunch but we Yanks feel guilty if we laze around for too long."

"I'm a house husband now, didn't you know?" He winked at Pearl. "The wife works hard to keep me in the manner in which I've become accustomed."

I laughed. Alexandre Chevalier was even wealthier than me, and that was really saying something. I kept my fortune a close secret, but Alexandre? Impossible. There were articles in magazines and national papers about him daily. Even Warren Buffet had mentioned what a good investor Alexandre was. He was supposedly the sixth or seventh richest man in the world. All from his own making. Unlike me. I'd had a leg up, a head start, because of my inheritance. We had something in common, though; money wasn't our motivation, ideas were, and their ultimate success.

We were all dining together under the stars. The hotel staff had laid a long table, especially for us, near the beach. Crystal wine glasses twinkled in the moonlight, and the women all looked glorious in their diaphanous gowns.

"I must say, ladies, you all look beautiful tonight," I said. "My very own brunette, a stunning blonde, and a gorgeous redhead. Who needs dinner when we have such a feast for our eyes?"

"The blonde is mine, so watch it," Alexandre joked.

"A man after my own heart," I said. He was as possessive as I was.

"I'm not after your heart, don't worry," he shot back, his wit a sharp tool. I could see why this man had done so well in business. He was astute and on the ball. With his French accent the word "heart" came across as "art." A double-entendre.

"So, gorgeous redhead," Pearl said, looking at Daisy, "it feels like years since I last saw you. Isn't that silly? But in fact it was only last month."

"Yeah, well, considering we speak every other day, I'm surprised you don't get bored with me. By the way, I forgot to ask, did you get your pearl necklace back? Had that loony stolen it?"

I noticed that Pearl shot Daisy a stony stare but Daisy's attention was on smoothing out her short, slinky dress, which my friend Jesse was paying careful attention to.

"What loony?" Will asked.

"That insane doctor who was looking after Daniel, you know, his own bloody sister-in-law," she said, as if it were common knowledge.

All eyes were on Daisy. When Janie tried to change the conversation, I really knew for sure something was up.

"Anyone for wine or are we all happy sticking with our cocktails?"

I nudged Janie's knee with mine. "Is there something you're not telling me?" I hissed at her politely, my gaze fixed. I remembered virtually nothing of my coma, but obviously a whole lot had been going on around me, and they knew things I obviously didn't.

"Uh, oh," Alexandre said.

"What?" Will asked. "Spill the beans."

And that's when I heard the story, or what I understood (by the shifty expression in Janie's eyes) to be a small *part* of the story. I knew there was more, and I was sure as hell going to find out later. For now, they told me how Pearl had brought her priceless choker to my deathbed—her lucky mascot that had, she was convinced, woken her up from her own life-threatening coma a few years before. The pearl necklace had apparently vanished, and Kristin denied having any part of it. But the way they spoke Kristin's name, a disgusted lift of the eyebrow, a pinched twist of the mouth, I suspected there was a lot more to the plot than anyone was letting on. I didn't want to disrupt dinner—after all, I had to think of Janie's dad— but I'd corner my fiancée later.

"I hope you get your choker back," I told Pearl, "and thanks for passing it my way, it must have done the trick." I didn't believe in that sort of hocus-pocus but Pearl obviously did, and I didn't want to offend her.

Pearl was silent. Alexandre cleared his throat, an embarrassed grimace sweeping across his face.

"Actually, um, we've tracked it down already," he said.

Janie's dad cut in. "Tracked it down. How?"

Pearl took a sip of her cocktail. "We'll talk about this later, after dinner."

What the hell was going on? "That's great, isn't it?" I remarked. "Did someone find it and call the police?"

"No. I developed a tiny, very tiny GPS tracker for jewelry and small objects," Alexandre explained. "It's not on the market yet, but it does work."

"Cool," Will said, his eyes wide. "How's it powered, what if the battery runs out?"

"It's solar powered," Pearl told us. "Accurate within five feet. You know, we developed it with dogs and children in mind, but now we've got it down to being so small, it's perfect for valuable art, jewelry and other priceless items."

"So, where is it, then?" Daisy asked.

Pearl winced. "On the neck of a rather elegant lady who was recently vacationing in Hawaii. We lost track and, um, well, her plane landed early this morning, and she's now in LA."

"My mother?" I asked, incredulous.

"I'm afraid so," Pearl said.

"Well at least you know she won't pawn it," I

joked. "Damn, that's shameful, to have your own mom turn out to be such a magpie. Well, I'll call her first thing tomorrow and make sure she gives it back. Who would have thought . . . my own mother! Had no idea she had the . . . what's the word? The—"

"Thank you, the fish looks superb," Alexandre intercepted politely. Two waiters had arrived, carrying a silver platter of fresh, barbequed fish. "This should be delicious, spiced with Chinese herbs and cooked the traditional, French Polynesian way," Alexandre said. "It's a dish they often serve for the bride and groom. And speaking of the bride and groom to be, I'd like to make a toast to Janie and Daniel. May they live long, happy, beautiful lives together, at each other's side, faithful, devoted, and with just a smattering of intrigue. I wish for you the same degree of happiness that Pearl and I have found together. To Janie and Daniel! Forever!"

Everyone at the table burst into applause, and I had to admit, Alexandre's little speech made my eyes smart. I quickly wiped away a pending tear, embarrassed that anyone should see me so emotional.

24

Janie.

I KNEW I was in trouble and that I'd have to explain to Daniel why I'd been hiding everything about Kristin from him. But it was time I came clean. He was suspicious as hell and I knew he'd hound the information out of me one way or another. On our way back from dinner, he pinned me against a palm tree, on the beach. Luckily it was dark so nobody could see. The stars were clustered across the Milky Way and the moon shone bright enough that I saw the glinting anger glittering in his eyes. He was pissed off, but the cocktails, the delicious dinner, and fun conversation had put him in a good mood.

"Now, Janie, I want an explanation, this second."

"It can wait, it's—"

"I said NOW!"

His breath was on my neck. There was a predatory, sexual hunger in the way his gaze dragged over my body, taking in the sinewy folds of my pink silk chiffon gown. He held my wrists in one hand and raised them above my head.

"Or I'll fuck the information out of you. Hard. Fast. I could get cruel." His mouth was lingering above mine.

My lips lifted into a little smirk. Daniel's "cruel" was my idea of fun.

"I'm not joking, Janie, I don't like secrets, they fucking well make me furious." A snap of his eyes, deeper now . . . his expression darkly dangerous.

A mixture of thrill and fear coursed through me. I found the "angry Daniel" sexy, but very scary too. Like when I was late for rehearsals and he chucked me out of the room, humiliating me in front of the cast, singling me out like a bad, bad girl, who had to stand in the corner. But there was always that sexual undertone which had me getting myself off the second I got home, imagining him and his hard cock ravaging me, even though he was a married man at the time and I knew I couldn't have him. All my dreams turned out to be true. He *had* desired me as much as I him. At least, I imagined so.

"Did you want me even when you were married?" I slurred. I was suddenly aware I was pretty darn tipsy. I leaned against the tree for support.

"Don't you dare try and change the conversation." His grip on my wrists was tight. "We're going to be married tomorrow, but I am *not* going to make vows if there's a fucking secret between us. Is that clear?"

Ouch. Sting. The idea of us not marrying felt like a lethal punch to the gut.

"I'll tell you," I said, "but I don't want you to get mad. So why don't we talk about it tomorrow when you're calmer?"

"Too late, I'm already mad. All because of you. Bend over." He loosened his hands so my raised wrists were free. His voice was ice. My heart raced.

"What?"

"Bend over, you need to be punished, obviously." His eyes were flashing like two deep pools of oil. Black, but reflecting glints of orange.

Heathcliff. Mr. Rochester locking his wife in the attic. Daniel spun me around so my back was to him and lifted my dress above my waist. "Bend."

I was so shocked I did what I was told. Although, I wondered to myself why I was about to marry a madman. I would spend my life being told off, bossed around, controlled . . . why was I about to sign up for this? Literally, I'd be signing a contract—a marriage contract.

"Daniel, I—"

"Don't speak!" His hand was making circles around my bare bottom. I hadn't worn panties as I didn't want any line to show. The slap came down hard on my right cheek and stung like anything.

"Ouch."

Then again, on my left cheek.

"You can't do this, Daniel! I won't allow it!"

"Get on all fours. Bad puppies need to learn how to behave with their masters, some sort of precedence needs to be set." I could tell by the tone of his voice that he was being ironical, half teasing, that he was playing a part, but it seemed as if this role had gotten under his skin. In one swift movement he took something out of his tux pocket then threw the jacket on the sand, under the palm tree. "Down."

"No." My smarting ass was still on show for the world to see, although the beach did seem empty—except for us and our crazy spectacle. Thank God it was nighttime.

"On your knees, Janie, I won't ask twice." I slowly got down on my knees, using his jacket as a blanket. I was a little wobbly, my head spinning.

"Okay, now tell me everything," he demanded, his hand poised on my butt for another round of slaps.

Why I was playing this silly game, I wasn't sure, but baiting Daniel was turning me on. Turning him on too. "No, I won't. Not tonight. Doctor's orders. You shouldn't get worked up."

He snickered. "And what do you think the doctors would say now if they took my pulse, eh, little minx? You don't think I'm worked up EVERY . . . SINGLE . . . DAY? You test my patience, Janie, you make my dick constantly hard. You don't do as you're told because you're stubborn and headstrong, and it makes me want to fuck you. No . . . makes me *need* to fuck you."

Daniel came down to my level, also kneeling. He changed his tune; whispered seductively in my ear and it sent shivers along my spine, hardening my nipples, making me wet. "Janie, baby, are you going to tell me what happened while I was in my coma? Every single detail?" His voice was soft and it made me groan when his finger trailed along the small of my back, down my crack, and down to the hot, beating pulse between my legs.

"Yes, but not tonight," I taunted, my tease a red flag to a seemingly calm bull before I knew he'd charge with fury. "We can discuss it all to-morrow when alcohol isn't flowing through our veins and we're both a little more *compos mentis.*"

"I'll give you compos fucking mentis." Before I knew what was happening, he'd handcuffed my right ankle to my right wrist. My balance was all over the place, especially after all those cocktails, and he had extra advantage because his anger had him focused.

Focused on me.

In seconds my left ankle was locked against my left wrist.

"You know what *esposa* means in Spanish?" he growled.

"Wife," I said, happy that I remembered some from school.

"And it also means handcuff. So watch out, little miss, because possessive fucked-up husbands have certain rights."

My crazy position had me trussed up like a Thanksgiving turkey. I had no choice but to either rock forward (exposing my ass even more) or lean back and try and sit on my haunches, but that was pretty uncomfortable. My arms were straight as sticks. "You're admitting you're fucked up, then?" I said with a titter.

"If I weren't fucked up, baby, you'd find me boring." He tilted me forward. "Now that's a very pretty sight, that little pink rosebud and that juicy wet cunt ripe for fucking."

I gasped, feigning shock at his bad language. "You shouldn't use crude words like that, Daniel," I warned, hardly in a position (ha, ha) to make demands.

"I never pretended to be a gentleman. What you see is what you get. You don't have to go through with this union if you don't want to. Are you in or out?"

I laughed. "More to the point, are *you* in or out?"

"You want me in?" His hands held my hips

still and his tongue swept up my wet opening. I moaned. Here we go again, I thought. I was still sore. This was madness. This man was madness, and I was obviously deranged for loving him so hard.

My view was upside down, my head on the sand as I peeked backwards between my legs. His shirttails were askew, his dress pants on, but the fly undone, his cock sticking out.

"This is going to hurt, baby," he said, ramming into me. It did hurt, but I welcomed the pain. I was his vessel and had no choice but to either scream for help and have him arrested for rape, or surrender to this onslaught of . . . of . . . overload. Yes, overload. Thanksgiving stuffing being crammed into a too small, bound-up turkey. Why was I enjoying this so much? What was wrong with me?

"Who are you?" I panted as he pumped me without mercy. His shaft reaching my G-spot and bringing me an overwhelming ache to climax—it wasn't long off now. This position was a welcome surprise. "I don't even know you," I groaned. I was helpless. At the mercy of this sudden stranger.

"I'm Finn," he rasped into my back. "Your

Dominant. Remember? Your co-star for *The Dark Edge of Love*? It isn't called the 'dark edge' for nothing, baby. So get used to it 'cause rehearsals have just begun."

25

Janie.

WHENEVER I DRINK alcohol I wake up, either in the middle of the night, desperate with thirst and can't get back to sleep, or very early in the morning. It was now five a.m. I glugged down nearly a liter of mineral water while Daniel slept conked out by my side. I felt antsy. Nervous about the wedding today, both excited and worried about my future with this man.

My wrists and ankles were lightly bruised. Not too bad because the handcuffs were softly lined, but still, I didn't feel like the typical bride on her wedding day, knowing what had happened last night. The "damage" between my legs hurt less than I had expected. Maybe I was getting used to his savagery? Hmm, worrying. Was he really just acting out a part? Or was this the secret Daniel, revealing his true nature, little by little? Was marrying him a risk? He certainly behaved like he owned me, yet he reveled in my independent spirit and feistiness and wanted me to be my own person. A contradiction. An anomaly. But then that was Daniel Glass in a nutshell. And whatever madness lurked inside him, whatever darkness, I was hopelessly in love with him and could never even imagine being with anyone else.

Last night we hadn't gotten around to my revelation/confession. After he'd unlocked each pair of handcuffs and carried me back to our room, he collapsed on the bed. He, too, was drunker than he thought. I took off his shoes and dress pants, covered him with the sheet, and he hadn't stirred since.

With one eye on him now, I slithered out of bed, padded to the bathroom, and closed the door so as not to wake him. Showered. Brushed my teeth, slipped on a simple shift dress and quietly left the room. A walk on the beach to welcome the sunrise would be good meditation, I decided.

Anything to prolong the inevitable. I was dreading his wrath all over again. Today was the wedding; there'd be no time for games or hanky-panky or even make-up sex. I had to fix things between us. And fast.

It was dark outside, the horizon brushed with a pale peach, but no sun yet. Still a few stars in the violet sky. I saw a lone figure striding along the beach. I was about to turn in the opposite direction but realized it was Daisy. I still missed our therapy sessions, even though she had pronounced me "quite cured" and strong enough to "move on alone."

The squeaky white sand was cool beneath my bare feet, the air breezy but not cold. I made my way over to her until she spotted me.

"Shit, you scared the living daylight out of me," she said with a start, her classy British accent even making the word 'shit' sound elegant.

"Sorry, couldn't sleep."

"That makes two of us."

We sat down on the sand and gazed at the lapping waves. The water was a shimmering turquoise, clearer than a swimming pool even so early in the day.

"Why couldn't you sleep?" I asked her.

She raised a ginger eyebrow. Her curly red hair was wild and unkempt, her nose already brushed with freckles from the sun despite only being here two days. I always thought of Daisy as rather beautiful. Irish roots. Pale skin, and big blue eyes. When I first met her she was a lot more curvy, but I noticed that she'd lost quite a bit of weight. She was still single—her husband had cheated on her way back when. I always wondered why she hadn't met someone special since him.

"I spent the night with Daniel's friend Jesse last night."

"No!" I squealed with girly delight. I'd barely even noticed him at dinner, he'd hardly said a word. "Well, he's very handsome, but obviously the strong silent type."

"Strong, yes. Not so bloody silent in the sack, I can tell you."

"So what are you doing up? Why aren't you still in bed with him? Oh right," I remembered, "Amy."

"No, Amy had a pajama party with Pearl's kids last night, it wasn't that."

"So, you snuck out?"

"He's bloody intense. Shags like a runaway train."

"So it was worth it, then? Or . . . not sure if that's a compliment or not . . . the runaway train bit."

"Great one night-stand, but no, I can't get into a relationship right now, I can't risk getting hurt again."

"But Daisy, it's been *years* since you had something serious, isn't it?"

"Yeah, and I'm all the better for it. Enough about me. What about you? Nervous? Excited? Daniel's besotted with you. It's written all over his face."

"He's . . . it's . . . I can't explain. He's wrong in so many ways, but I'm in love with him, so what can I do?"

Daisy dug her feet into the sand. "Well, yeah, I haven't forgotten you droning on and on about him when you were doing *Where The Wind Blows.*"

"That bad?"

"A broken record." She laughed. "Just joking. Of course I didn't feel that way about you, I was your therapist, but now we're friends I'm allowed to tease, aren't I? Don't lose your sense of self though, Janie, your autonomy. You know what Pearl once told me? And I've never forgotten it—advice from her dad. He told her, 'Pearl, whatever happens, whatever you do, even if you end up with someone wealthy, you always need to have your own 'fuck-you' money. Money that's just yours that you can do what you like with. Women need to have their own fuck-you money at all times. You never know when you'll need to catch a plane or treat yourself to something special.' I memorized those words and they've served me very well."

"He's right," I agreed. "I'll keep that in mind." Despite Daniel's wealth, I was determined to continue working, no matter what. I loved my independence and knew that he was the type of person who could devour a woman if she didn't hold her own. I would never let that happen to me.

We sat there, watching the waves in silence, my mind turning over the events of the past few weeks.

"Something's plaguing you, Janie. What?" After all those years of therapy with Daisy, she knew me so well.

I told her everything that had happened while Daniel was in his coma. Kristin arranging for me to be locked up, the lab break-in with Sophie and Elodie, the tortured animals, the fact that I hadn't told Daniel because I didn't want to rile him up, that the doctor's had warned me to keep him calm.

Daisy frowned. "That's a big burden you're carrying on your shoulders. A bloody big secret to be keeping from him, especially when he was quite the protagonist, and especially when he's about to be your husband."

"What do you mean, 'protagonist?'"

"Well, he was unaware—out cold—but all the drama centered around him, so don't you think he has a right to know? Especially as you're about to walk down the aisle with him."

I felt myself biting my lip. "I know. You're right. I should get back to our room now and face the music."

"Yes, you should." She was quiet for a beat, a smile smoothing away her frown. "So what's your gown like?"

"A really simple white linen dress. Nothing swanky. I figure I want Daniel to see just me, not my outfit, not my hair and makeup. Just me: Janie. Barefoot. We're having our ceremony on the beach, Tahitian style. On the beach with a Polynesian priest, in front of an altar decorated with local flowers, under the coconut trees."

"Sounds perfect," Daisy said. "Can't wait." The waves splashed our feet, washing up tiny pebbles and shells that glinted in the dim dawn light. I could hear the heavy crash of more distant waves on the barrier reef. This place was paradise. "Well, as much as I'd love you to stay and watch the sunrise with me," she continued, "you'd better get back to Daniel or he'll think you've done a runner on him. Good luck. And if you need a hand with any of the arrangements, call me."

"The hotel's doing everything. My only job is to show up."

"Clever you. My wedding was a nightmare," Daisy admitted. "Stress City. Planet Stress, actually. Wish I'd had your foresight. By the way, isn't Star Davis meant to be coming? Or is that just rumor?"

"They came in late last night. You'll meet her and Jake today."

"Well, I hope the paparazzi haven't got wind of it or it'll be a total fiasco."

"They checked in under a different name and Star's unrecognizable right now. She's playing a lesbian boxer in her next movie and looks like a

boy. Her long blond locks have been hacked off."
I stood up. "Thanks for the pep talk, Daisy. I'll remember that advice about the fuck-you money, too."

"See you later alligator." She grinned. "Sorry, that's what comes of being a mom."

"In a while crocodile. I look forward to having kids, it must be fun."

"Really, you're ready? You're so young still."

"As soon as *The Dark Edge of Love* is done, I'm up for it." I brushed the sand from my dress, surprised by what I'd just said. *I was ready to have kids? Really?*

Yes, yes, I was. I was ready for everything and anything with Daniel Glass.

Except for now. I was nervous about telling him the truth of what had happened when he'd been in his coma. Mainly because of the secrets I'd been keeping from him, rather than the information itself. Secrets guarded far too long. I don't know what I'd been thinking hiding everything. It seemed the only thing to do at the time, terrified he might go and die on me—fear overriding reason. I hoped all hell wouldn't break loose.

After all, we had a wedding to attend.

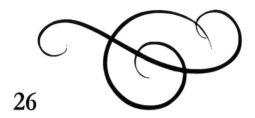

26

Daniel.

I AWOKE TO an empty bed. Janie gone. Panic spiked my alcohol soaked veins. Drinking like that had been really dumb. I never drank cocktails. A whiskey or a great cognac, yes, but *cocktails*?

She'd changed her mind, obviously. I'd behaved like a fucking asshole last night, playing around with those handcuffs. I'd *spanked* her? Yes, I had, the memory suddenly clear. What had I been *thinking* doing something like that the night before our wedding? Did my outrageous behavior concerning my hungry libido have something to do with my coma? Usually coma patients lose their sex drive, but one of the doctors had warned me that hyper-sexuality, although rare in men or women, is a well documented side-effect of neurologic disease. Lesions of the orbital parts of the frontal lobes may remove moral and ethical self-control and lead to "indiscriminate sexual behavior," he'd told me.

Hmm, I wondered.

I showered, drank all the water and soft drinks from the mini bar I could lay my hands on, and felt instantly better. It was very early, not even six a.m. Janie's cell phone was lying by the bedside table—a good sign, she hadn't packed her stuff. Yet. The idea of us not marrying had me on the bed, head in hands, tears welling in my regretful eyes. I'd fucked her. Not made love to her like my beautiful bride-to-be, but *fucked* her. Defenseless. Handcuffed. What had gotten into me? My mind scrambling for answers, I recalled why I had been so worked up. The conversation at dinner. That's right, Janie had been harboring secrets.

Still, no excuse for my behavior.

The door opened. My fiancée tiptoed in but then caught sight of me sitting on the edge of the bed, naked, looking like that Rodin statue, "The Thinker." She rushed over and kneeled, burying her head in my lap. The last thing in the world I wanted was for my dick to stand to attention, but of course it did, having her head so close to my groin. As usual, it was out of fucking control.

"Just ignore that son of a bitch," I said. "He's incorrigible. And getting between us."

"Getting between me," she joked.

"I hadn't meant that to be funny." I smiled weakly. I didn't want to screw things up. I had to get things right with Janie, just had to. I wanted to grow old with this woman. Wanted to sit on a park bench and feed pigeons with her, one day. Or squirrels. Or whatever pensioners did. I was in this for the long term. Till death do us part.

I stroked her hair, threading my fingers through her soft locks, cupping the delicate shape of her scalp in my hands. She was so little, so vulnerable. And I was such a brute. *Beauty and the Beast.* "Please forgive me," I whispered, bowing my head to hers. "I don't know what came over me last night. Did I hurt you?"

"A bit."

"Sorry, baby."

"*I'm* sorry," she replied.

This was the moment, was it? When she'd

weep and tell me she couldn't go through with it? "What are you sorry for?" I asked softly. "You're about to bear me bad news? Tell me you don't want to marry me?"

"No, don't be silly." Her sweet words made my solar plexus take a leap. "I was keeping secrets from you," she told me.

The next couple of hours we sat out on our terrace above the water, and did nothing but talk. I stayed calm throughout, even though some of the things Janie revealed made me feel as if my heart were burning coal-fire. The whole Natasha memory was dredged up because of what Kristin had done. They were so very alike, not just physically but in the way they used people. I had forgotten just how much Natasha had wounded me. Not so much because I was in love with her, but the betrayal factor. The trust. Believing someone cared for me when the only thing she wanted was my money, and what she could extract. She had sucked me dry. Devoured my blood like one of those tropical leeches. And now I was hearing nasty details about Kristin, it was doubly painful. As if Natasha had risen from the dead and was taking everything dear to me and trying to destroy it. Destroy Janie.

Janie told me about how she had been locked up in some basement, next to Kristin's goddamn laboratory. The anger I felt inside was beyond any emotion I had ever experienced. Poor Janie, terrified, not knowing if she'd live or die, while that stupid wannabe actor probably did a good job of scaring her shitless. I listened on to Janie's tale, willing myself not to explode. Each second got worse. She explained how Alexandre's sister Sophie, and her daughter Elodie had intervened, and how they'd discovered that Kristin had wangled her way into getting power of attorney from my mother (thanks, Mom, for letting me know), obviously in preparation for my planned death. At one point, Kristin was even pretending to Janie we were married. Fucking lunatic. I'd fire that little weasel of a concierge who worked at my hotel, for starters. Throw him out on the fucking street and make sure the only work he got was scrubbing toilets. Janie's story got even worse; by the time she'd told me about her own hospitalization, I couldn't take anymore. She'd been through hell and back, and I'd been oblivious all this time. Worse, I'd handcuffed her last night, after she'd been *abducted*, only a couple of weeks before! I felt just horrible.

"Say something," Janie said. "You've suddenly gone all silent."

"I just can't believe someone can be so malevolent, so malicious." *And how I could have been so insensitive.*

"She's obviously crazy, actually deranged. There are people like that in the world. Who function perfectly on one level—you know, her success as a doctor and things—but are actually mentally unstable in other areas of their lives. She's a wacko and should probably be locked up."

A dark thought flashed across my unforgiving brain. I didn't want the woman locked up, I wanted her dead. Out of the picture for good. She was a danger to Janie—I couldn't risk having her lurking in the shadows, even if Elodie was tracking her whereabouts via the Internet and her cell phone. That was no guarantee. Elodie would get bored, sloppy, forget about Kristin because she'd have better things to do with her life. What if Kristin reemerged one day, seeking revenge? Her torture of animals compounded it all. Vivisection had been something I had avoided thinking about all these years—the subject too polemical—but Janie's descriptions of what had been done to those poor creatures made my insides roil. At least that part of the story—the knowledge that they'd been taken to a sanctuary—had a happy ending. But the woman was a cold-hearted monster.

"So she was using me—my brain—as fodder for her medical findings?"

"That's what it looked like except she denied it, of course, said she was measuring your dreams. And worst of all, her colleagues seemed to support anything she said or did. Her reputation flawless. She'd even won some award for best doctor of the year."

"Fucking sicko."

"Daniel, I know this is horrendous, but can we try and put this all aside for today and concentrate on our wedding? Maybe you understand why I wanted to keep it from you until you were better. Please don't be angry with me, I was desperate, didn't know what to do. So scared you'd lapse back into your coma if you became upset. Please understand."

"I can't understand. I can't understand how that woman can be so rotten inside."

"Please."

I held Janie's hands in mine. "You have my word. No more talk today—nor while we're here—about that bitch and how she tried to ruin our lives. We're stronger than that. But I want a promise from you?"

"What?"

"Promise me first."

Her reply was tentative. "Okay."

"That I will deal with this when we get back, in my own way, and I want no questions and no objections as to how I choose to do it."

"Don't ask me about my business," Janie said, quoting Al Pacino in *The Godfather*.

I feigned a small smile. "Exactly."

27

Janie.

DANIEL KEPT HIS promise and didn't say another word about Kristin.

Our ceremony was perfect. He loved that I was dressed so simply and admitted that he'd been worried that I'd "do" myself up too much. He preferred me with little or no makeup, loved my long white linen dress that was devoid of any designer label. "After all," he told me, "I'm marrying a woman, not a dress." I think, after Natasha, glamour turned him off.

All I had to do was show up at our bungalow in the late afternoon. A pair of local Tahitians wearing garlands of Tiare Tahiti flowers arrived at our little dock, one paddling the traditional canoe, the other strumming a ukulele. While the canoe waited for me, two Tahitian girls and two boys knocked at my door. They laid a white garland of this national flower—a sort of Gardenia—around my neck, its heady aroma, mixed with anticipation, made me almost dizzy with excitement. They settled me into the canoe, helping me balance myself, and I was paddled off toward the shore, where Daniel, Dad, and our guests were waiting.

Dad helped me out of the canoe, his proud face holding back tears. "You look like your mother on our wedding day," he told me. "But even more exquisite."

It was twilight. There were lit fire torches flickering along the beach, the white sand now golden, and white flower petals had been sprinkled in a pathway, serving as our wedding aisle. Dad and I linked arms and slowly walked toward my groom. Daniel was also dressed in white linen, barefoot. His wayward dark hair and golden tan made his eyes glimmer the brightest blue—I had never seen a person look so happy. So relieved. One of the boys who had come to our bungalow blew into a conch shell, a rumbling low baritone that sent sound waves across the beach.

I surveyed our little crowd, their happy smiles a blur. Will, Pearl, Alexandre, Daisy, Star, Jake, Jesse, and the bevvy of children chitchatting and excited by the spectacle.

Dad led me to Daniel and we joined hands.

"You're the most beautiful woman in the world. And that's a fact," Daniel said in his no-nonsense director's voice.

"And you the most handsome man I've ever laid eyes on," I gushed.

The priest, also donning a garland of flowers, began the ceremony. There was music, more ukulele and some soft drums. The priest tied palm fronds on Daniel's right wrist and my left wrist, and we held hands tightly as he poured ocean water from a conch shell over our joined hands. This symbolized new life. Then one of the girls handed us each a leis and floral crown, which symbolized responsibility.

"My queen," Daniel said with a wink, placing the wreath atop my head.

"My king," I replied, making the same gesture.

We exchanged vows and our little crowd applauded. I felt as if I were slightly suspended in the air, a few feet off the ground, but then the words, "I now pronounce you husband and wife" brought me back down, and I sensed the silky sand between my toes, the dappled light of the late evening sun on my shoulders, slightly shaded from the coconut trees above us.

The evening whirled past as if it were a dream. Dancing, music, excited, squealing children running along the shore, splashing on the edge of the water, and then dinner under the French Polynesian stars, which were more luminescent than ever. I felt stronger inside, knowing that whatever troubles lay ahead of me, I had a husband by my side. My husband. Daniel. Daniel Glass. I was aware that it wouldn't be easy, but it would be an interesting journey, never boring, always a little edgy. But there was one clear thing: this man loved me for everything I was, my weakness, my strength, my foolishness, my pridefulness. And he saw something in me that I did not: perfection.

I was perfect for *him*.

He made love to me that night, worshipping my body, tears of happiness in his eyes as he trailed kisses across my shoulders, my neck, my nose. In fact, I think he covered every inch of me, all the while telling me how happy I made him, how we were in this for life, how I must never feel alone again, that he would catch me if I fell.

Before going to bed I slipped quietly into the bathroom and did a home pregnancy test—I bought one at one of the airport pharmacies *en route*. I'd had a suspicious feeling something was up, because of my breasts feeling swollen lately. Besides, I realized I was late for my period.

Positive. I was pregnant!

Does it sound corny to say this was the happiest day of my life? Because it truly was, especially when what was to come next shattered us into thousands of little pieces.

Perhaps having Glass as my last name was some kind of omen.

28

Daniel.

I HAD GONE through hell with Natasha, I deduced, to be able to truly appreciate heaven with Janie. There is no Yin without the Yang. Sad, but true. Without the shit you don't get to really *feel* happiness the same way.

Our wedding was fucking perfect.

This waif of a girl had conquered my heart. Something deep in my subconscious had known that she was one in a million the day she walked into my rehearsal room that time.

My Janie Juilliard was all mine.

But I never imagined she'd break my soul in two. Never courted the possibility that anything or anyone could come between us. Thought our strength of love was unbreakable. But when you have Glass for a name, I guess a happy ever after was asking too much.

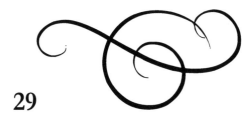

29

Janie.

I T WAS THE blood test that started it all. That simple blood test that I was so looking forward to; the one that would confirm the little pink line of the home pregnancy test.

I whipped into the office of the closest gynecologist to where Daniel and I were staying. Daniel had rented a house in Laurel Canyon. I hadn't even asked him to come along with me to the doctor. It would be a speedy, whip in, whip out visit. On my first visit, the day before, it was. They just took my blood, but when I went back the next day to get results, it took a lot longer than I anticipated.

The doctor was a wiry young man with spectacles, who looked more like a librarian than a doctor. All I had imagined was a quickie chat, nothing more. Had I thought about it, I would have asked to see a woman.

But forty-five minutes later, after he had noticed, with the ultrasound, that my liver was enlarged, he examined the results of my blood work with an eagle eye.

"Your blood work is very concerning," he told me, his brow a deep furrow, his glasses slipping to the end of his bony nose. He perused the results, his eyes scanning up and down. "I know this is hard to hear, but better now than later, right? I always like to be up-front with my patients. I'm afraid it looks as if we're dealing with some type of blood cancer. Your white cell count is abnormally high. Maybe Leukemia."

I didn't believe him. Not for a second. I almost laughed in his face. Served me right for not going to Star's doctor, for picking some random physician, based on the proximity to our rental place.

"There must be some kind of mistake," I said with confidence, not trusting his diagnosis one bit. "I've been hospitalized twice in the last month.

Once in LA, and once in Las Vegas. They did blood work. I was diagnosed as anemic. Nobody said anything about cancer."

His forehead creased into a crinkly map—veins like rivers. "They did a CBC? A complete blood count?"

"Of course. And nobody alerted me to the fact I was anything other than anemic." His words, and mine, echoed in my head. Back and forth. The Big C. No way! A mistake. It had to be. *They would have known if I had freaking cancer!*

"We'll conduct a bone marrow biopsy, just to be sure. Not here, but at the hospital. I don't have the resources, and it's not my expertise. Don't lose hope, Janie, there is excellent treatment at hand, especially if you have an extensive insurance policy. Of course, if you *do* have cancer your best hope to beat it is a termination."

My heart plummeted to the floor. "Of the baby? You mean an *abortion*?"

"You're very young. And that's the problem with cancer in young patients. Because of your "health" and vigor, the disease spreads at an alarmingly fast pace. Were you in your seventies, say, there'd be the luxury of more time to combat it because cancer is slow in older patients. But the fact you're pregnant, with all your hormones in full swing, so to speak, the disease can develop at an alarmingly fast pace. We simply can't wait around until after you've had the baby to start treatment. Chemo can hurt the fetus—there's a risk of the baby being born premature."

He'd said *an alarmingly fast pace,* twice. Yes, I got it the first time. Why hadn't I brought Daniel with me? What *was* all this? He'd know what to say, what to do. I still couldn't believe this gynecologist was speaking like an oncologist . . . as if he were a cancer expert. How dare he? How dare he turn my life upside down?

"I'm . . . I'm leaving. I need to speak to my husband," I rasped, gathering my purse and the results from the test. "And get a second opinion. I'll be in touch."

THE NEXT COUPLE OF WEEKS were like wading through a wet and dangerous marsh plagued with malaria-borne mosquitoes. Never letting us rest, nor relax, nor revel in the happiness of our marriage, for one second. Always nipping at us, threatening death and demise.

Acute Myeloid Leukemia, that's what I had. AML is a pretty rare form of cancer that affects the blood and bone marrow, causing an overproduction of immature white blood cells that can't fend for themselves. It's very unusual for someone of my age. I learned that typical symptoms of AML mimicked anemia due to a lack of red cells; causing persistent tiredness, dizziness, paleness, or shortness of breath. All of the things I'd been suffering from when it was thought I had anemia. Daniel threatened to sue both hospitals for their harmful misdiagnosis, but we needed to conserve our energy to the problem at hand, not "cry over spilt milk" as Daisy so aptly described it. I had to make decisions, remain strong. Everyone was supportive and wonderful, yet I didn't want to spend time with anyone except Daniel. Not my father, not Will, nor any of my friends. This was our private battle, not some soap opera. I didn't want sympathy, and I certainly didn't appreciate judgment when it came to my personal decisions.

I became more and more determined that I would not sacrifice my baby, not go through with a termination. Daniel tried to remain calm, but he let me know I was his number one priority and that we had a whole life ahead of us—plenty of time for getting pregnant again. But he had his facts wrong; it was possible that the treatment could cause infertility and this was my only chance. Daniel wasn't pushing me, but made it clear which way the wind blew for him. I felt differently. I had always been pro-choice, yet suddenly when it was *my* baby, my life, and Daniel's life right *inside* of me, there was no way I would deliberately harm our creation, our living and breathing child. I couldn't.

I'd take the risk. Call me crazy, but that was what I decided to do.

30

Daniel.

I'D BEEN BLAMING the hospitals, not comprehending how two major institutions could have misdiagnosed Janie's disease, mistakenly thinking it was anemia. But as I was scanning the Internet for as much information as possible about Acute Myeloid Leukemia, a realization slapped me hard across the face. I read:

> **In most cases the causes of AML remain largely unknown but it is thought to result from damage to one or more of the genes that normally control blood cell development.**

Damage. The image of that *witch* resurfaced. The film that Star had captured on her phone: Kristin hovering over my brain like a vulture. Kristin fucking Jürgen . . . still at large. I'd been so focused on Janie, I hadn't had time to even find out where she was.

I rolled her name on my lips like poison: Kristin fucking Jürgen.

I thought back. Janie was diagnosed as suffering from anemia when she was admitted to the hospital in LA. Ditto when she ended up collapsing from exhaustion at the hospital where I lay in a coma. Kristin had gotten in to her room, no doubt. Had she administered some sort of drug, using Janie like one of her lab animals? The way she'd been using me? What if she had injected her with something that had set off the disease? Leukemia was often found in people living near telephone towers, or where there were radiation leaks. Chemicals in cigarettes, hazardous substances like asbestos—these had been proven to set the cancer in motion.

I scoured the Internet frantically.

I read everything I could about induced cancer in lab animals and came across the chemical Benzene, still used widely in manufacturing. It said:

Benzene is known to cause cancer, based on evidence from studies in both people and lab animals. The link between benzene and cancer has largely focused on leukemia and cancers of other blood cells.

I read on:

Benzene has been shown to cause chromosome changes in bone marrow cells in the lab. (The bone marrow is where new blood cells are made.) Such changes are commonly found in human leukemia cells.

benzene

'bɛnziːn/

noun

noun: **benzene**

a colorless volatile liquid hydrocarbon present in coal tar and petroleum, and used in chemical synthesis. Its use as a solvent has been reduced because of its carcinogenic properties.

But could it induce cancer within a matter of

weeks? I couldn't find any evidence to the contrary, nor evidence supporting this theory. Yet what a clever way for Kristin to test her experiment! She wouldn't even need to be present herself, she'd hear soon enough if Janie had fallen ill. Janie was an actress, and about to be a big star—or would have been had this not gotten in the way. Obviously we had suspended filming *The Dark Edge of Love.* Kristin could have administered the Benzene, or whatever poison she'd used, sit back and see what happened over the course of the next few years.

I took a deep breath to compose myself. Looked up at the blue, LA sky. Tried to get a grip on my spiraling emotions. Maybe my imagination had run wild. Maybe I was lashing out at anything, anyone to blame for Janie's illness? My accusation was pretty crazy. For starters, what was in it for Kristin besides a morbid curiosity?

I wouldn't say a word to Janie about the ramblings in my head. What was the point in piling on more angst, more worry? And it sounded fatalistic, the idea of some lethal, carcinogenic chemical being injected intravenously into an innocent patient by a mad doctor. It would terrify Janie.

What was done was done—we needed to find a cure, not dwell on the how and why. I needed to be her rock, not some lunatic making the situation worse. We had a team of fantastic oncologists who were treating Janie. The best money could buy. There was hope, they all said. We were going to beat this together.

But the idea of that evil woman Kristin still on the loose made my gut roil.

I called Alexandre Chevalier to get Elodie's number. He didn't ask any questions but simply said, "The good doctor? You'll find Elodie has dealt with that."

I didn't reply but knew exactly what I had to do.

And I needed to do it sooner rather than later.

WHILE I WAS AWAY I'd arranged for Janie to stay at Star and Jake's beautiful house on the beach in Malibu. It was perfect for my wife. Full-time staff on tap, company for Janie (because Star wasn't working right now), a chef, a chauffeur to drive Janie to the hospital every day for her chemotherapy, and anything else she needed. We had just moved into our place in the Hills—a rental—

until we found the house of our dreams. Well, this had been the plan until all this happened. I didn't want Janie to be alone up there, and having her father and brother come to stay would hardly be relaxing for her. She needed rest and plenty of care. Star's place was perfect for a few days.

I felt bad leaving my wife, but I couldn't take my mind off my ex sister-in-law, and something had to be done. Elodie had tracked Kristin to where she said she'd be: Bermuda. So far, it seemed she hadn't broken the rules; she was lying low, keeping her face down. But I didn't trust her an inch. No, make that a millimeter. I wanted to talk to her, face to face. Look into her eye. Sit her down and discuss every minute detail of her experiments, and grill her about her activities in the hospital while Janie had been admitted. I needed raw facts to stop myself fantasizing about the maybes, the possibilities of what she'd done or was capable of doing. She was a respected doctor, a neurologist. Was she really a certifiably insane person too? So far, all I was going on was Star's little film, which proved nothing conclusive. Although locking Janie up was hardly behaving in a normal, rational way. But I needed to talk to other specialists, Kristin's colleagues, as well as to her. Leave no stone unturned before bringing her to justice. I'm an impulsive man, but I am also fair. I didn't want a rash decision, based only on emotions, to haunt me for the rest of my life.

Elodie refused to let me know where I could find Kristin. Of course, I did my own research but couldn't come up with a damn thing. For all intents and purposes, Kristin was invisible. That was the first surprise. I deduced she must be going under a new name. Was Elodie aware of this? I guessed she was. It made me nervous that I was putting my trust in this strange young woman, who couldn't have been any older than Janie. She was an odd bird, Elodie. A loner. I met her very briefly when I woke up from my coma. We'd Skyped a couple of times since, about Kristin, but other than that I barely knew anything about her, apart from what Janie had told me; she was Alexandre Chevalier's niece, but not by blood. Sophie Dumas was technically her stepmother. She was a bit of a genius with technology. A hacker. A backpacker who'd traveled in unsavory, dangerous countries, and who refused to take advantage of her wealth. In short: a bit of an enigma.

I'd offered to put Elodie up at the five star resort, where I was staying by the ocean, all expenses paid, but she refused.

We arranged to meet for lunch by the pool there, and when she arrived at my table, I almost didn't recognize her. She had a hollow look in her eyes—beautiful—but like a specter of a girl. She wore all black—skinny jeans and a sleeveless tank T-shirt, and her slim frame denoted a worked-out physique like someone who practiced martial arts. A tomboy, except her long brown hair, of no distinct shade, allowed her femininity to shine through.

She dumped a backpack on the chair beside me. "Sorry I'm late, I got held up." Her accent unmistakably French, but her confidence with the English language showed she'd mastered the nuances of meaning. "Let's get a couple of Cokes and go for a walk. Can't be too careful."

"Fine," I agreed.

She said little else, just made small talk about the warm weather, the pretty views of "the sea," (they're not used to oceans in Europe), and how much she had enjoyed getting to know Janie in Vegas. "You're a lucky man."

"Beyond lucky," I said, not letting on about the Leukemia.

We drank our sodas and she got up. I took her backpack but she snatched it from me. "There's a lot of cash in there," she said coldly.

Maybe what Janie suspected was true. That Elodie was a real-life, modern-day Robin Hood hacking into people's bank accounts and transferring great sums of money into more deserving ones. She smiled at me as if what she'd said was a joke. I bet it wasn't.

After the beauty of Bora Bora, the beach seemed nothing special. Funny that; you can get so spoiled by luxuries in life. Bora Bora, I supposed, could never be matched, considering it had been thus far the highlight of my life, marrying Janie there.

"So," I began, "tell me where she is."

"She's gone," Elodie answered, her eyes fixed on mine.

"What? What the fuck! I thought you knew exactly where she was!"

"Oh, I do. Don't worry, she's not going anywhere."

This was crazy. One minute Kristin was

"gone" and now she wasn't "going anywhere."

"What exactly do you mean? Elodie, I *need* to see her."

"You can't."

"Then why the hell did you bring me out here?"

"I didn't bring you out here, you brought yourself."

I was beginning to think something was getting lost in translation, after all. "Look, Elodie, I really need to talk to the woman. She's dangerous, as you know. I don't want to lose tabs on her. I need to get to the bottom of what she did and make sure she won't . . . look, she's a loose cannon, she—"

"She's dead, Daniel. And disappeared. Like, 'evaporated' disappeared. Melted, if you like, like the Wicked Witch of the West in *The Wizard of Oz*. She doesn't exist anymore."

I remembered Alexandre's words, "You'll find Elodie has dealt with that." I hadn't paid any attention to their significance. I'd seen movies where they used acids to "melt" bodies. Hell, I'd even seen that on TV—*Breaking Bad,* for instance—but the idea of it actually happening to someone I knew, however monstrous they'd been, and the thought of someone as innocent looking as Elodie having anything to do with it . . .

"You had her *killed*?" I asked, incredulous. I'd had fantasies of getting rid of Kristin, but now that Elodie was being so cold blooded . . .

The corner of Elodie's lip lifted as if of its own accord. "She won't be bothering anyone again. You know what? She'd volunteered at the hospital here in Bermuda. Can you believe it? 'Helping out,' playing nursie. She was up to her old tricks again. Bad enough, but you know what *really* made me move my ass down here and do something about her, once and for all?"

I shook my head. My imagination had already been stretched as far as I thought possible.

"She took in a stray cat. Fed him with treats, lured him into trusting her with saucers of milk. And the next thing you know? The bitch had put electrodes on his head for her sick little experiments. I've got her on film. My spyware caught all sorts of shit. People like that, Daniel, simply don't deserve to live."

I was speechless. I thought of Janie. And of my own narrow escape. And all Kristin's patients over the years, including her very own sister. But now I'd never find out. Never have the chance to know for sure. All I could come up with was, "Where's the cat now?"

Elodie smiled. A real smile that showed her teeth and made dimples in her cheeks. It was the first time I'd seen her look genuinely happy. "I'm taking him back home with me. I've named him Luckster."

31

Janie.

I COULD GO into details about the next six months, but I won't. People don't really want to know about the nitty-gritty details of what it's like to be a cancer patient. They pretend they do, nod their heads in sympathy, but are too embarrassed to ask questions and really *talk* about it, or they give you *that look*, which is even worse. As I said, pity was the last thing I needed—or wanted.

I lost the baby. Nobody would confirm whether or not it had anything to do with the chemo. I also lost my hair and looked uncannily like Natalie Portman in *V Is For Vendetta*, because I shaved my head completely, joking that I should audition for a part in a Sci-fi movie or join Star as her lesbian boxer sister.

The Dark Edge of Love was postponed indefinitely. I begged Daniel to "rehearse" with me—I'd learned all my lines—but he always refused. Thought me too fragile. I wanted to be strong and fearless, but my body was pale as mottled marble, and weak.

Daniel had bought us a house, not far from Star and Jake's, overlooking the ocean in Malibu. I watched surfers from my bedroom window, my bruised legs and arms wishing they could ride with the waves like the limbs of those I lived through vicariously every day. My attention span got shorter and shorter, and simple things like reading a book became a huge chore. Daniel would read to me: poetry, and my favorite children's books, but even his melodious, rich voice had me falling asleep mid sentence. I couldn't concentrate on TV . . . everything and anything became exhausting. I hadn't eaten for days. Something as basic as swallowing felt like climbing Everest. Daniel would lie with me, his warm body trying to heat up my icy feet, in vain. He joked that I was his favorite flavored popsicle, but sometimes I caught him with tears in his eyes:

He knew I was dying.

There had been the never-ending question of his dinner date that he still hadn't given me an answer to. It was time for him—and he knew it— to let me know, once and for all.

I tried to say something, but my voice was so wafer-thin, Daniel had to bring his ear to my lips. "So, tell me," I whispered, "tell me who your dinner date is."

"You're the only dinner date I want. You, Janie, will always be the queen of all dinner dates." I felt a tear trickle down his cheek, and as he brushed his face toward me, I tasted its saltiness on my parched lips.

"That's cheating," I croaked. Letting him choose me as his dinner date was admitting death. I had to be strong for him. "You promised, you—"

"Shakespeare, then. Or Leonardo da Vinci . . . I don't even care anymore. Please, baby, I just want dinner with you." His voice was cracking. He took me in his arms—I felt like a loose sack of brittle bones—and he hugged me close.

"You have to choose," I whispered on a sigh, not letting him off the hook.

"Jesus," he said, finally. "Because he can work miracles."

I allowed my eyes to flutter shut. I had my answer, at least. Clever choice . . . Jesus could do a Lazarus on me.

"Do you know what it's like to love so much you think your heart is actually going to burst?" he asked me the next morning. Light was filtering through our floor-to-ceiling windows. I tried to sit up but all I managed was a little lift of my head. Daniel lay a large hand behind my bony skull, the other on my coat-hanger shoulder and hitched me higher. I sank back into the cushions he'd put there for my comfort, heaving an almost breathless sigh.

"No," I whispered, only just getting my words out, "because my heart is made of glass. Glass doesn't burst, it breaks." I let my eyes fall closed. Prisms of morning rays filtered through my lids . . . to my brain.

It was the last time I saw such a blindingly bright light.

So white, so brilliant, it . . . quite literally . . . took my breath away.

EPILOGUE.

Daniel.

I SAT STARING at the ocean, my eyes straying to the horizon. Staring out the window where my beautiful Janie had lain dying. Life goes on, I told myself. Life goes on.

Four years had passed since then. Four years, where so much had changed.

Our cat Luckster purred like a Porsche as he pawed my new wife's long brown hair, now tangled in his claws. I hadn't imagined a wedding could be more perfect than my union with Janie in Bora Bora, but I was wrong. I was in love, and getting married again to the woman of my dreams had made me feel more alive than ever. Especially as she was pregnant.

My wife laughed, prizing the cat's paws from her thick, healthy mane. It was good to see her really laugh, nothing made me happier.

Janie.

MY GLASS HEART didn't break after all. And Daniel's also remained intact. I found out that glass can be pretty tough.

The most dramatic scene I'd ever played in my life had a happy ending. By some miracle, I began to get better. Slowly at first, but soon at *an alarmingly fast pace*. My recovery happened as quickly as my demise. It was after Elodie came over to say goodbye when I was on my deathbed, bringing with her—and leaving behind—one of the cats that had been rescued from Kristin. One that hadn't had his voice box removed. A wiry tabby Elodie had named Luckster. He stayed by my side night and day, purring in my ear, using his warm body to wrap around my neck like an exotic scarf.

Luckster healed me. Nursed me back to health.

I say it was the cat, but Pearl attributes her pearl choker to being the miracle cure. Daniel's mother brought the necklace back, horrified that she'd been given stolen goods by Kristin, and Pearl made sure it lay under my pillow.

As for Kristin herself . . . well, she had a poetically just ending. Eaten by sharks, the papers said. Her body was never found, but they discovered a pile of her clothes on the beach, near where she lived in Bermuda. Death by drowning, the news proclaimed, her body gobbled up by fish, they surmised.

Daniel proposed to me again after I recovered. I laughed, but he was serious. Said I was like a "new wife," and that he wanted to renew his vows. So we had a blessing in a church in Venice, Italy. My gown was medieval style, blooming just below the bust line to accommodate my swelling belly. Yes, I was pregnant. Three years and counting, with the cancer in full remission. The chance of it coming back was so slim my oncologist told me, that I was in the all clear to "procreate like a rabbit," if I wished. Music to Daniel's ears. He took the doctor at his word.

For my wedding gift Daniel gave me a glass perfume bottle from ancient Egypt, which he bid for at auction against the top museum curators of the world. Iridescent blue—not so different from the color of his eyes—a priceless artifact to remind us both that glass can last forever. Glass can stand the test of time. Glass is not just beautiful, but resilient.

Daniel set Will up in business, looking after some of his stocks and shares. With Will's aptitude for numbers he's done extremely well for us all. *And* the multitude of charities Daniel founded, telling me that he owed a big one to "That Guy Up There."

Dad comes to visit us in LA often and has even contemplated moving here, to be near his grandchild.

I gave birth to our beautiful little boy last month. His name is Gabriel. Like the angel. He looks like a mini Daniel except he has my smile. He weighed a healthy eight pounds, and I now know what his dad was talking about; loving someone so much you think your heart is actually going to burst. Every time I look at Gabriel I feel this way. My family is my world. Eventually I will go back to theatre and movies, when I'm good and ready—I'll work hard for that coveted Tony and Oscar that I know are within my reach. But for now, all I want to do is hang out with my loved ones.

As for *The Dark Edge of Love,* it has been permanently put on hold. Daniel told me we need at least thirty years more "rehearsal time."

We're still working on several scenes.

Thank you so much for choosing *Hearts of Glass* to be part of your library and I hope you enjoyed reading it as much as I enjoyed writing it. If you loved this book and have a minute please write a quick review. It helps authors so much. I am thrilled that you chose my book to be part of your busy life and hope to be re-invited to your bookshelf with my next release.

If you haven't read my other books I would love you to give them a try. The Pearl Series is a set of five, full-length erotic romance novels. If you'd like to know more about Star and Jake, you can read their story in *The Star Trilogy*. I have also written a suspense novel, *Stolen Grace*.

Books #1 and #2 in The Glass Trilogy:
Shards of Glass (The Glass Trilogy #1)
Broken Glass (The Glass Trilogy #2)

The Pearl series:

The Pearl Trilogy bundle

(the first three books in one e-box set)

Pearl & Belle Pearl

(books 4 and 5 in one e-box set)

Shades of Pearl

Shadows of Pearl

Shimmers of Pearl

Pearl

Belle Pearl

The Star Trilogy

Stolen Grace

Join me on Facebook

(facebook.com/AuthorArianneRichmonde)

Join me on Twitter

(@A_Richmonde)

For more information about me, visit my website

(www.ariannerichmonde.com).

If you would like to email me:

ariannerichmonde@gmail.com

A Thank You Note from Arianne

This book has been a collaboration of sorts. My incredible beta readers helped me weave this tapestry of drama and intrigue with their clever observations and eagle eyes. Nelle l'Amour, my best writer friend, as always, has been my sounding board . . . what would I do without my Nelle?

Thank you Sam, Cheryl, Paula, Lisa, Gloria, Kim, and lovely Letty, for your spot-on notes, and for being so incredibly supportive. And everyone who has bought my books and recommended them to friends and family, or blogged about them to their followers, another massive thank you. Because of you I keep writing.

Made in the USA
Middletown, DE
03 July 2016